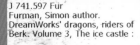

W9-BYJ-369

DRAGONS
RIDERS OF BERK

VOLUME THREE

THE ICE CASTLE

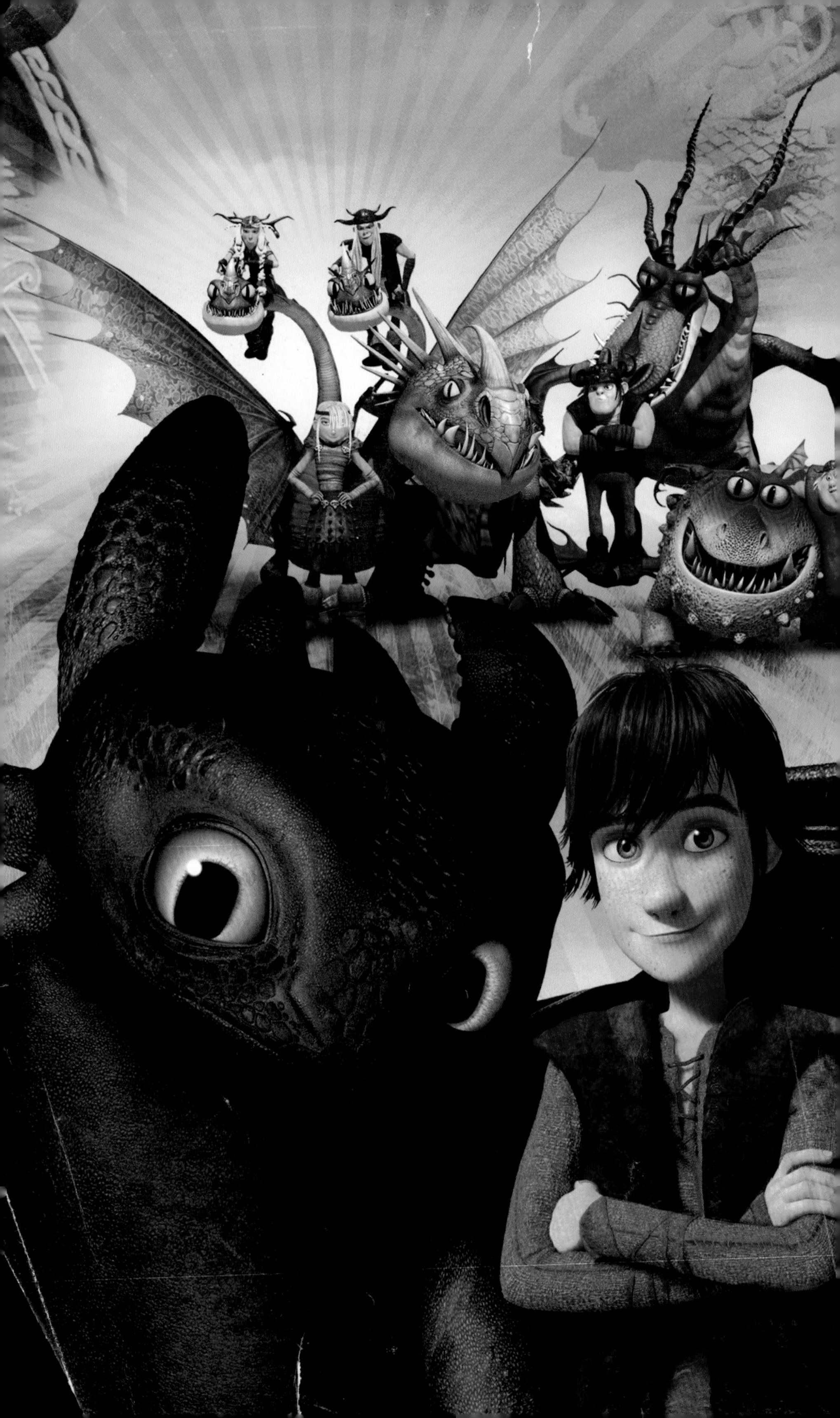

DRAGONS RIDERS OF BERK

VOLUME THREE

THE ICE CASTLE

SCRIPT
SIMON FURMAN

ART
JACK LAWRENCE

COLORING
DIGIKORE

LETTERING
JIM CAMPBELL

TITAN COMICS

DREAMWORKS DRAGONS
RIDERS OF BERK

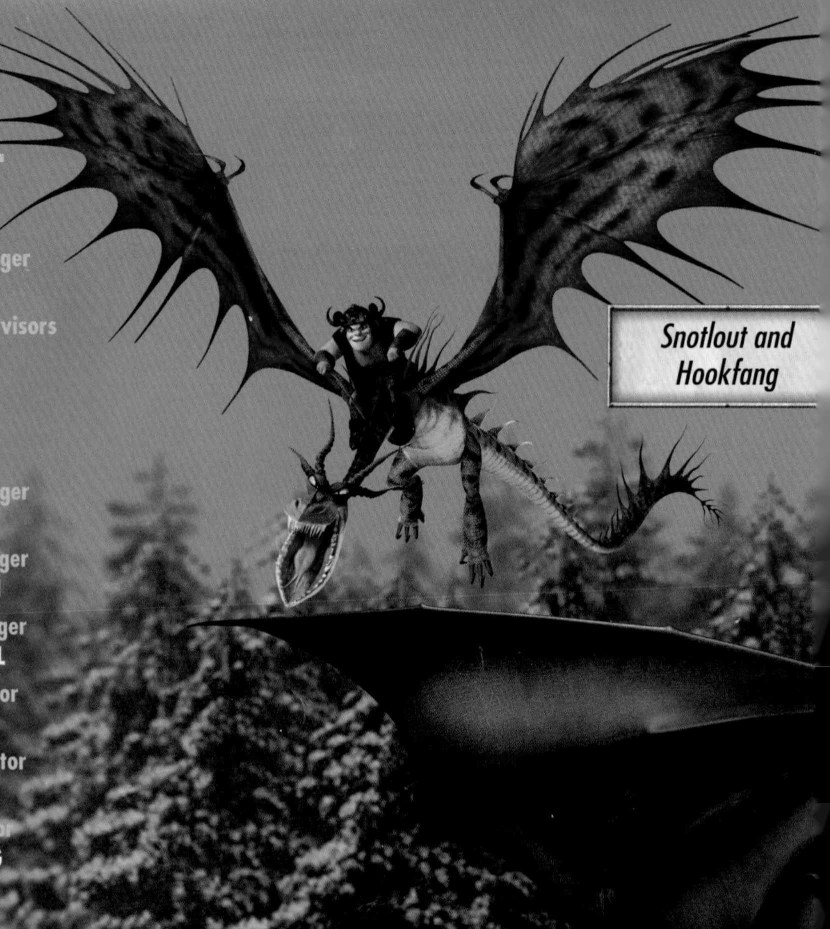
Snotlout and Hookfang

TITAN EDITORIAL

Senior Editor
MARTIN EDEN

Production Manager
OBI ONOURA

Production Supervisors
**PETER JAMES,
JACKIE FLOOK**

Studio Manager
EMMA SMITH

Circulation Manager
STEVE TOTHILL

Marketing Manager
RICKY CLAYDON

Publishing Manager
DARRYL TOTHILL

Publishing Director
CHRIS TEATHER

Operations Director
LEIGH BAULCH

Executive Director
VIVIAN CHEUNG

Publisher
NICK LANDAU

ISBN: 9781782760788
Published by Titan Comics,
a division of Titan Publishing Group Ltd.
144 Southwark St. London, SE1 0UP

10 9 8 7 6 5 4 3 2 1
First printed in China in January 2015.
A CIP catalogue record for this title is available from the British Library.
Titan Comics. TC0160

Special thanks to Corinne Combs, Alyssa Mauney and all at DreamWorks.

It's time to visit Berk, the home of Hiccup and his dragon, Toothless, plus Hiccup's friends who practise at the Dragon Training Academy! And let's not forget all the other Vikings and dragons…

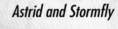
Astrid and Stormfly

Tuffnut and Ruffnut
& Belch and Barf

Fishlegs and
Meatlug

Hiccup and
Toothless

PLUS
*Stoick (Hiccup's father)
& Gobber*

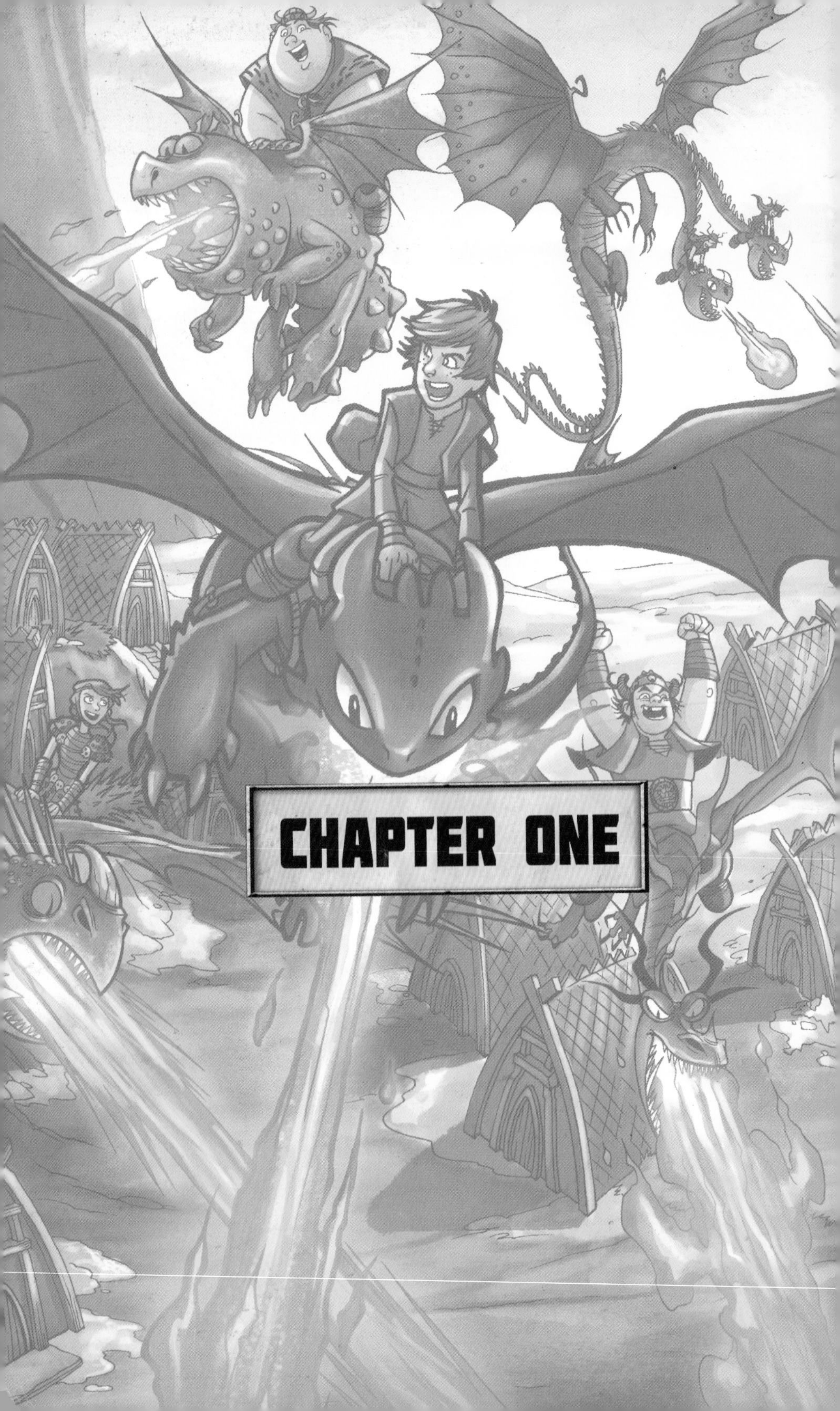

CHAPTER ONE

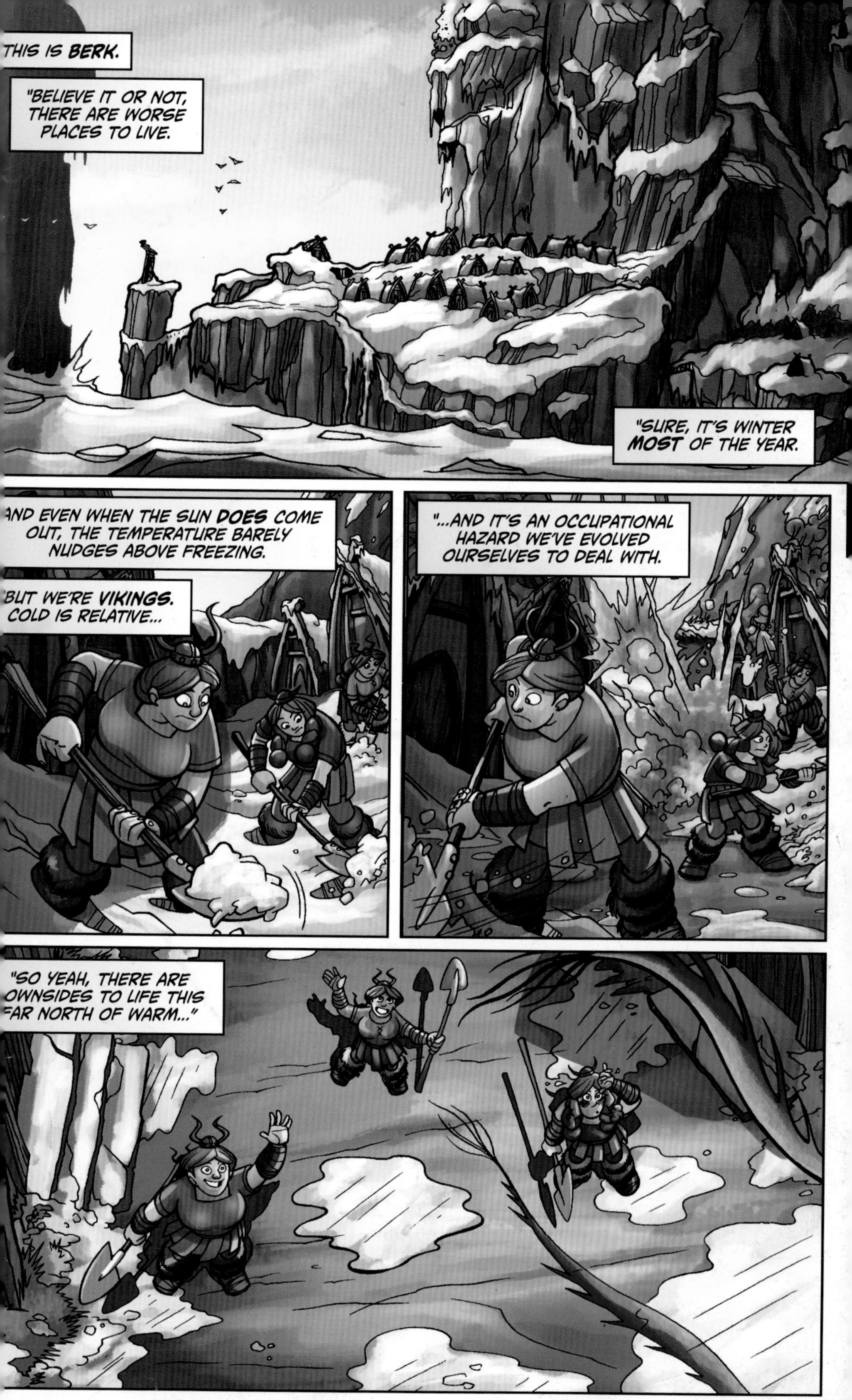

THIS IS **BERK.**
"BELIEVE IT OR NOT, THERE ARE WORSE PLACES TO LIVE.
"SURE, IT'S WINTER **MOST** OF THE YEAR.
AND EVEN WHEN THE SUN **DOES** COME OUT, THE TEMPERATURE BARELY NUDGES ABOVE FREEZING.
BUT WE'RE **VIKINGS.** COLD IS RELATIVE...
"...AND IT'S AN OCCUPATIONAL HAZARD WE'VE EVOLVED OURSELVES TO DEAL WITH.
"SO YEAH, THERE ARE OWNSIDES TO LIFE THIS FAR NORTH OF WARM..."

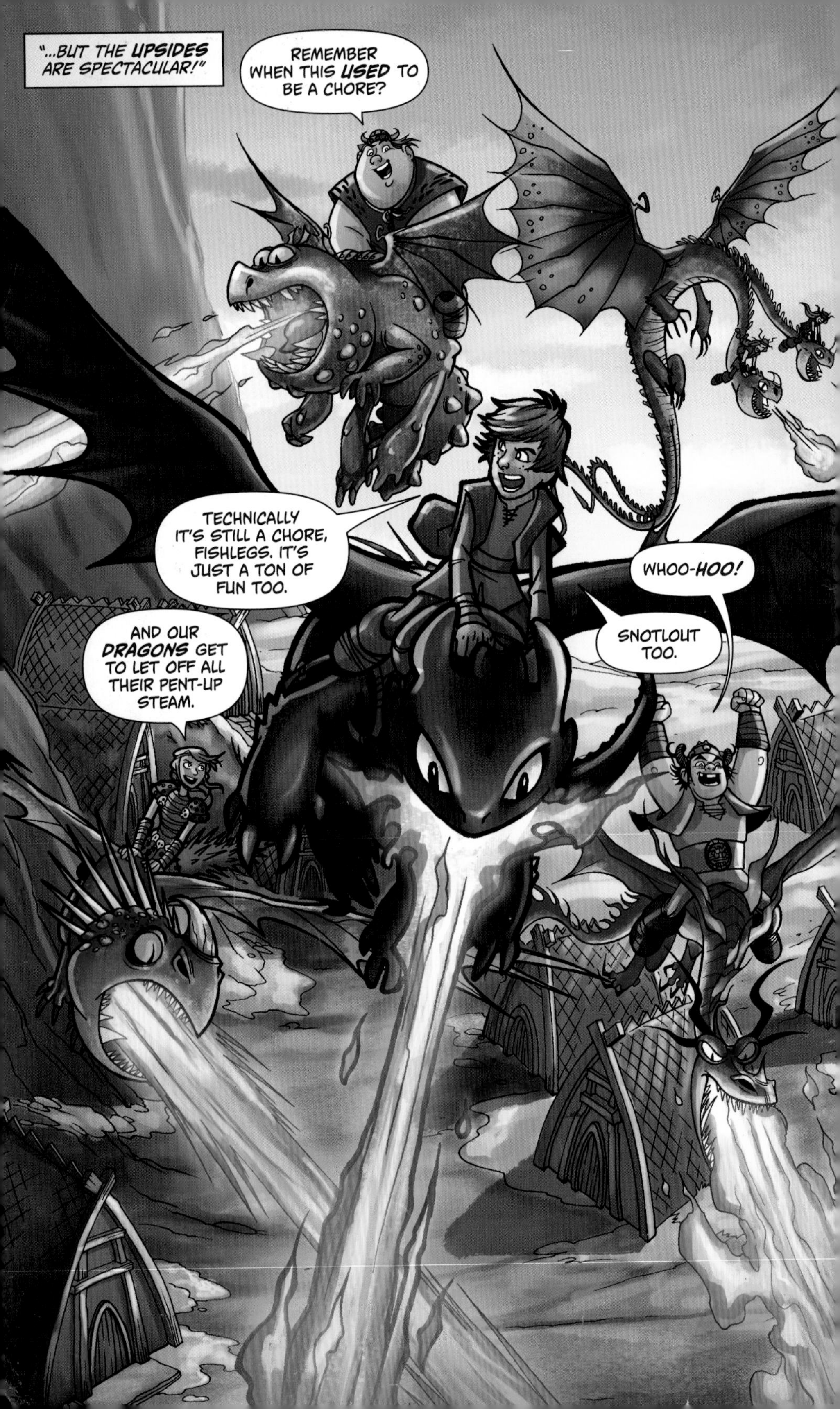
"...BUT THE UPSIDES ARE SPECTACULAR!"
REMEMBER WHEN THIS USED TO BE A CHORE?
TECHNICALLY IT'S STILL A CHORE, FISHLEGS. IT'S JUST A TON OF FUN TOO.
AND OUR DRAGONS GET TO LET OFF ALL THEIR PENT-UP STEAM.
WHOO-HOO!
SNOTLOUT TOO.

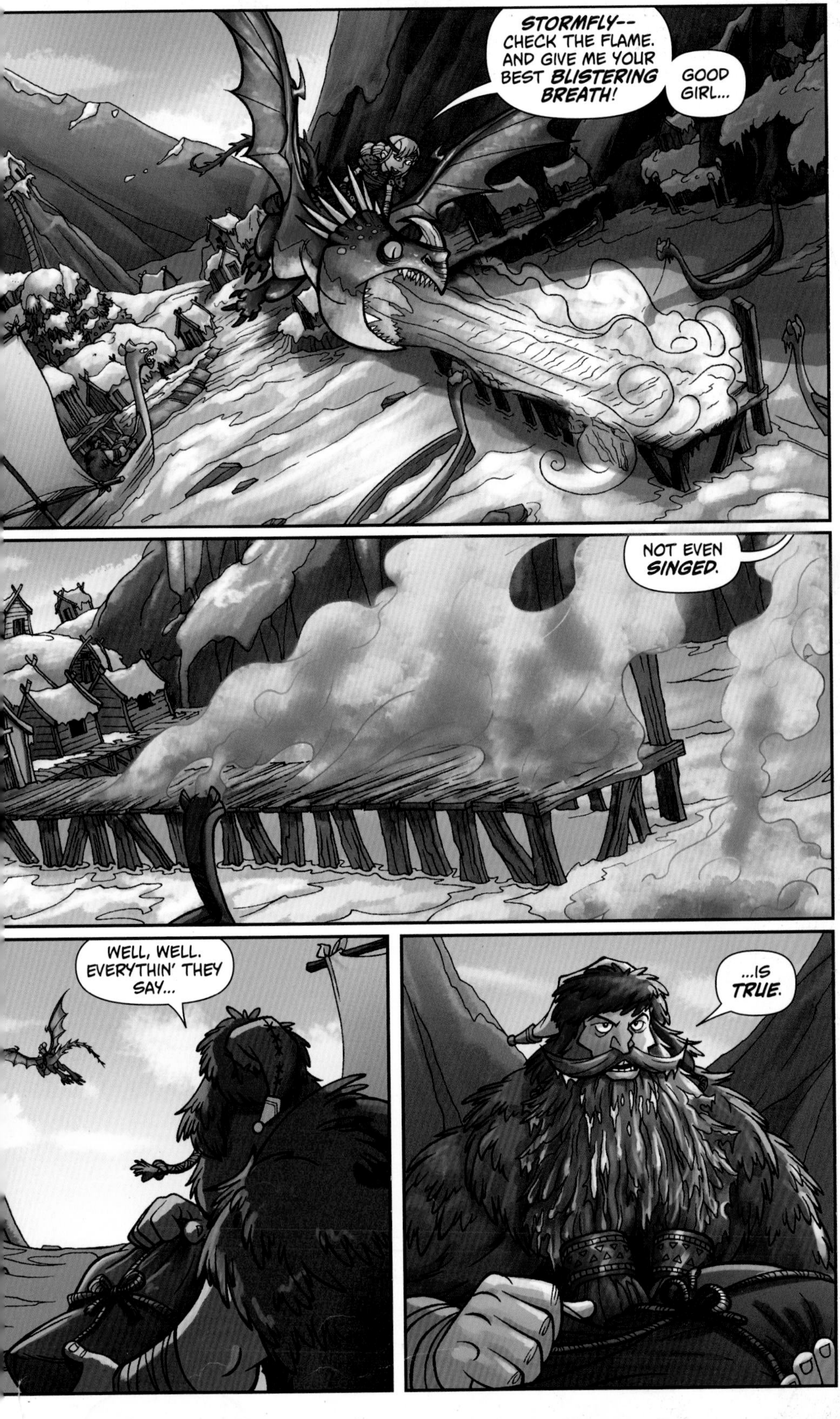
STORMFLY-- CHECK THE FLAME. AND GIVE ME YOUR BEST BLISTERING BREATH!
GOOD GIRL...
NOT EVEN SINGED.
WELL, WELL. EVERYTHIN' THEY SAY...
...IS TRUE.

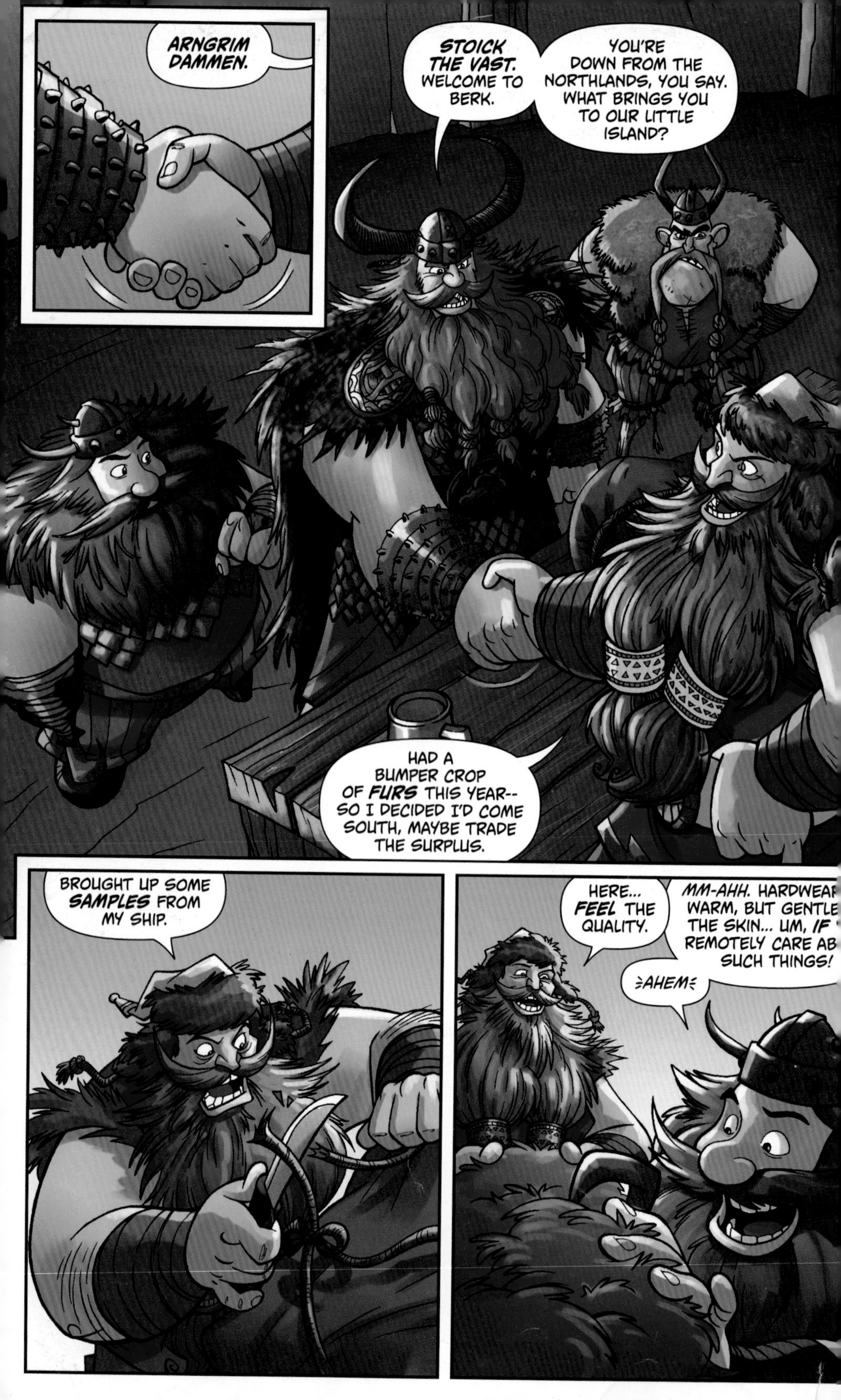

ARNGRIM DAMMEN.
STOICK THE VAST. WELCOME TO BERK.
YOU'RE DOWN FROM THE NORTHLANDS, YOU SAY. WHAT BRINGS YOU TO OUR LITTLE ISLAND?
HAD A BUMPER CROP OF FURS THIS YEAR-- SO I DECIDED I'D COME SOUTH, MAYBE TRADE THE SURPLUS.
BROUGHT UP SOME SAMPLES FROM MY SHIP.
HERE... FEEL THE QUALITY.
MM-AHH. HARDWEAR WARM, BUT GENTLE THE SKIN... UM, IF REMOTELY CARE AB SUCH THINGS!
AHEM

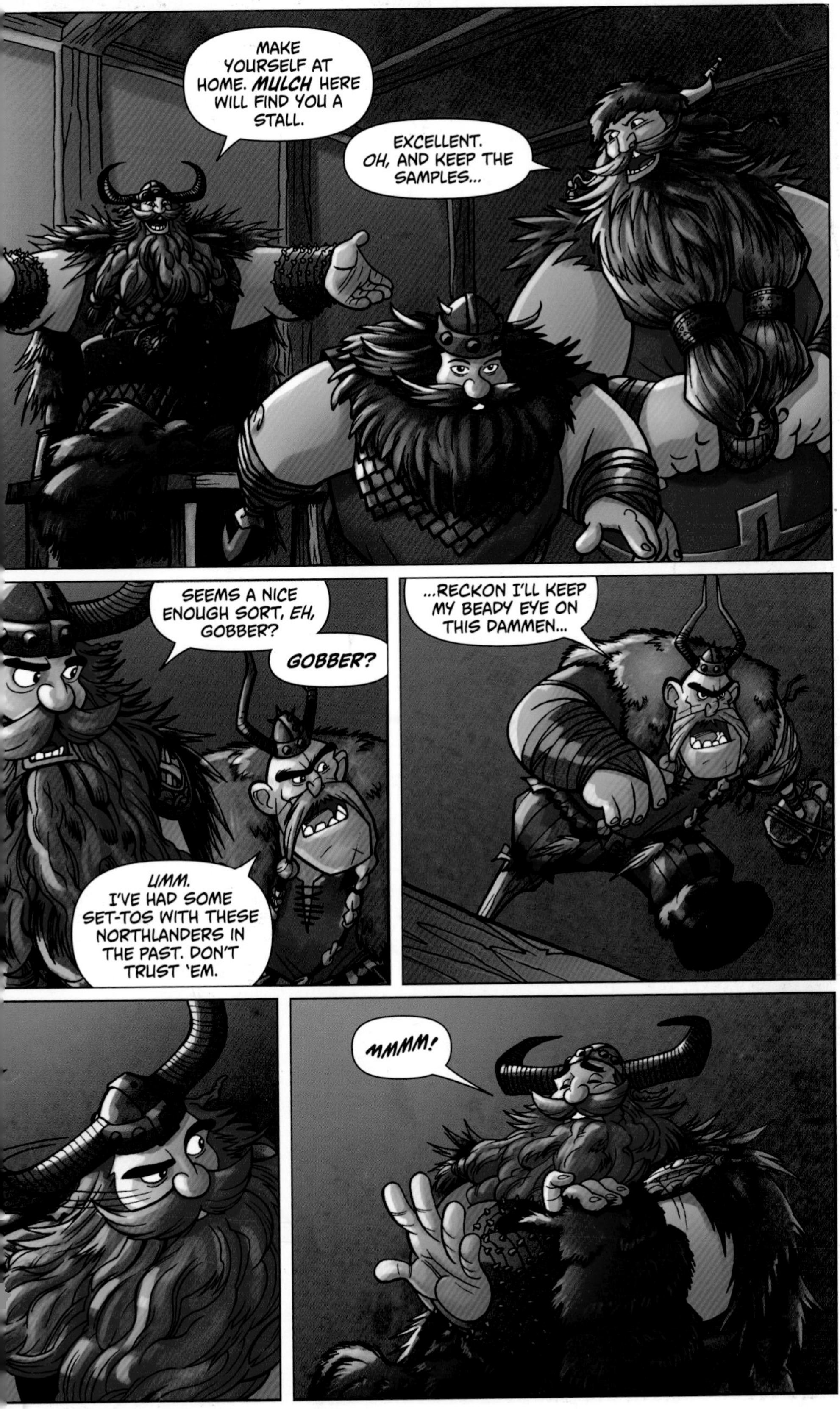
MAKE YOURSELF AT HOME. MULCH HERE WILL FIND YOU A STALL.
EXCELLENT. OH, AND KEEP THE SAMPLES...
SEEMS A NICE ENOUGH SORT, EH, GOBBER?
GOBBER?
UMM. I'VE HAD SOME SET-TOS WITH THESE NORTHLANDERS IN THE PAST. DON'T TRUST 'EM.
...RECKON I'LL KEEP MY BEADY EYE ON THIS DAMMEN...
MMMM!

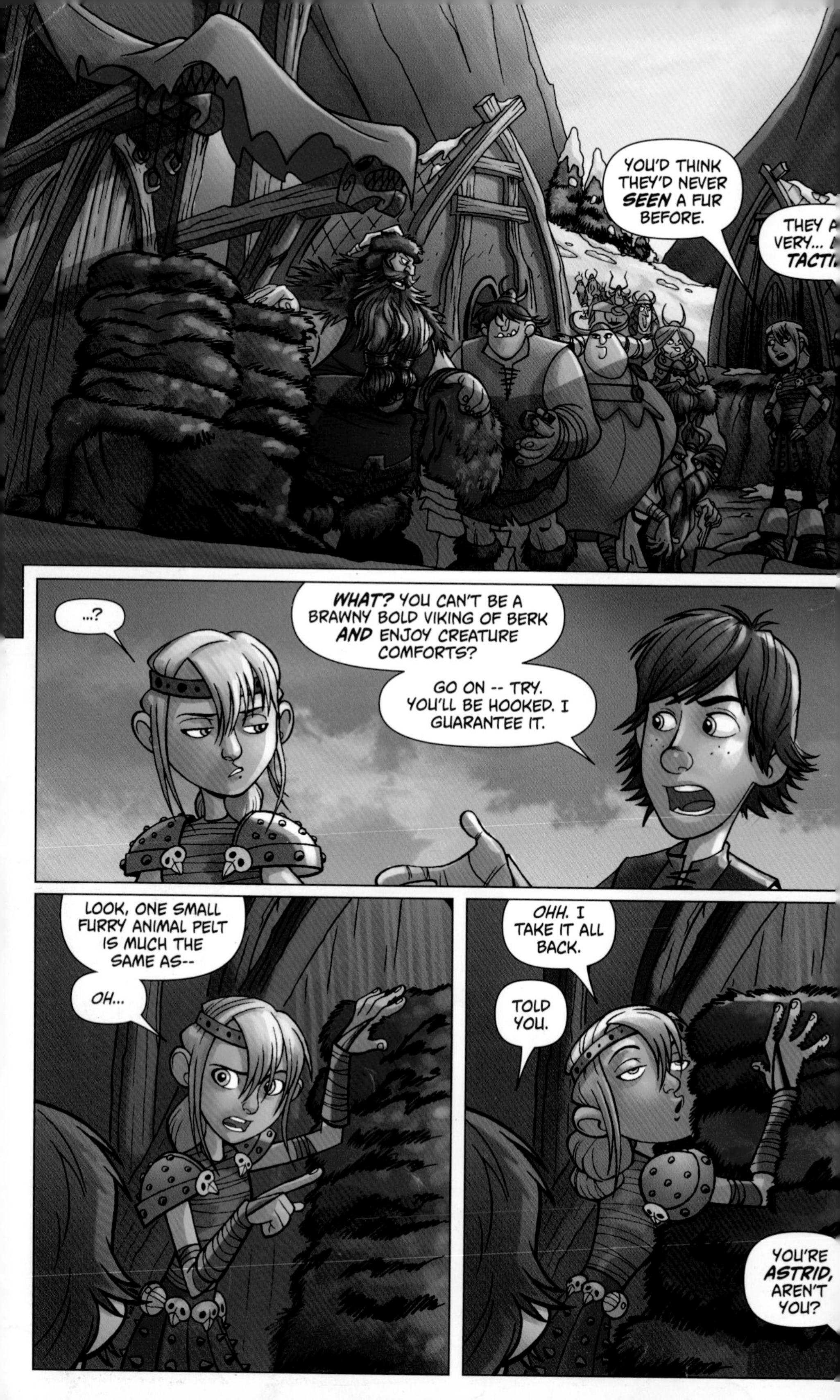
YOU'D THINK THEY'D NEVER SEEN A FUR BEFORE.
THEY A VERY... TACTI
...?
WHAT? YOU CAN'T BE A BRAWNY BOLD VIKING OF BERK AND ENJOY CREATURE COMFORTS?
GO ON -- TRY. YOU'LL BE HOOKED. I GUARANTEE IT.
LOOK, ONE SMALL FURRY ANIMAL PELT IS MUCH THE SAME AS--
OH...
OHH. I TAKE IT ALL BACK.
TOLD YOU.
YOU'RE ASTRID, AREN'T YOU?

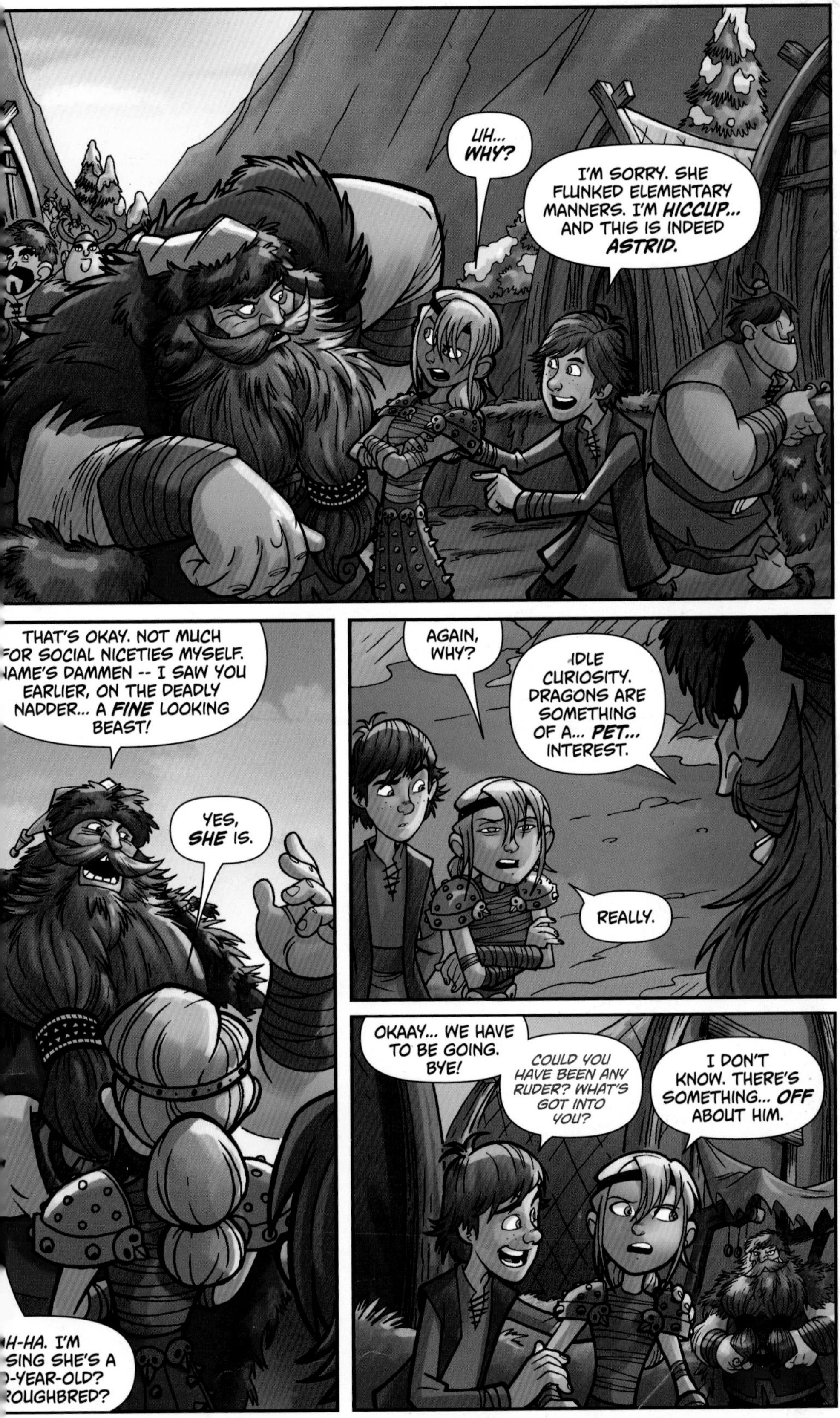
UH... WHY?
I'M SORRY. SHE FLUNKED ELEMENTARY MANNERS. I'M HICCUP... AND THIS IS INDEED ASTRID.
THAT'S OKAY. NOT MUCH FOR SOCIAL NICETIES MYSELF. NAME'S DAMMEN -- I SAW YOU EARLIER, ON THE DEADLY NADDER... A FINE LOOKING BEAST!
YES, SHE IS.
H-HA. I'M SING SHE'S A -YEAR-OLD? ROUGHBRED?
AGAIN, WHY?
IDLE CURIOSITY. DRAGONS ARE SOMETHING OF A... PET... INTEREST.
REALLY.
OKAAY... WE HAVE TO BE GOING. BYE!
COULD YOU HAVE BEEN ANY RUDER? WHAT'S GOT INTO YOU?
I DON'T KNOW. THERE'S SOMETHING... OFF ABOUT HIM.

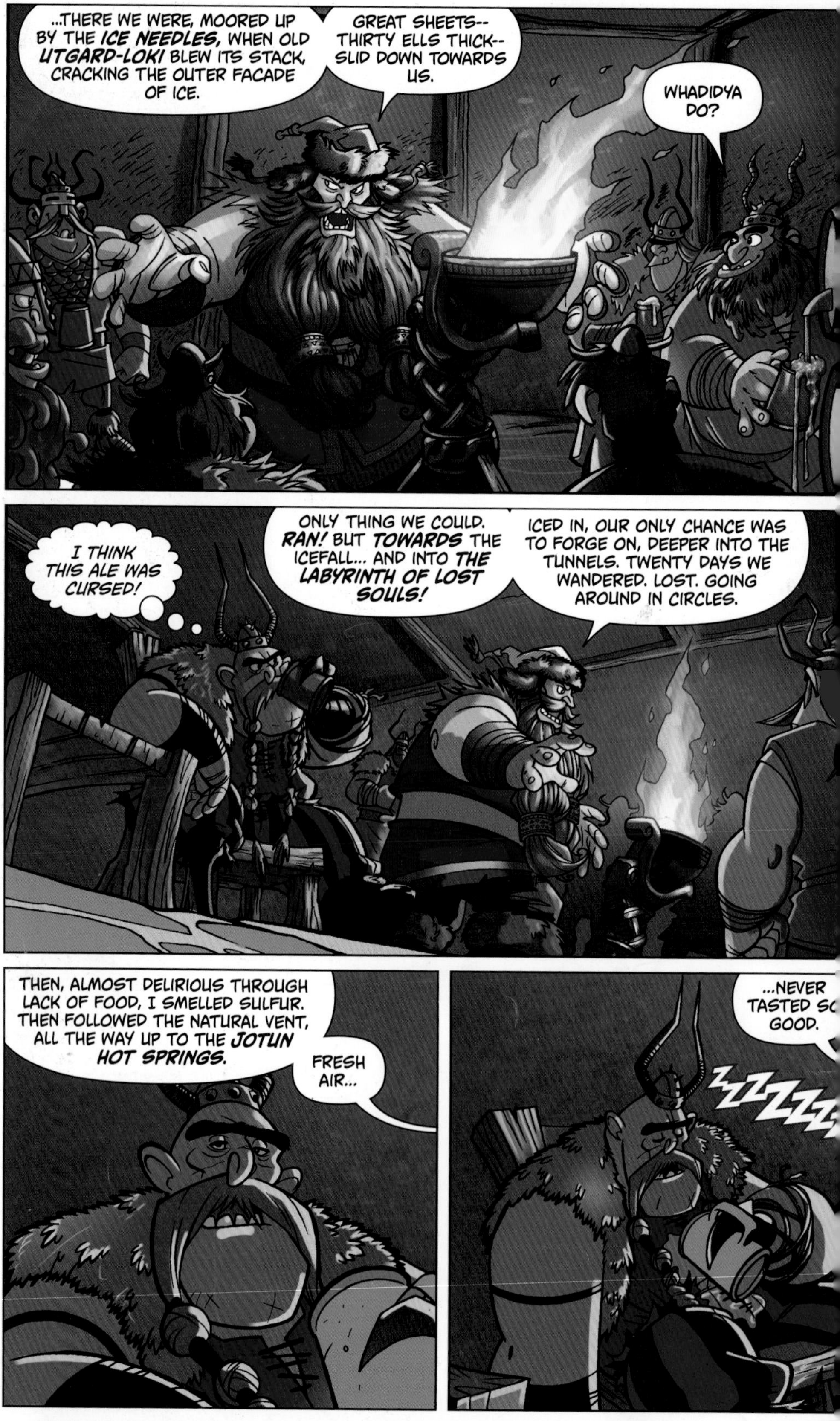
...THERE WE WERE, MOORED UP BY THE ICE NEEDLES, WHEN OLD UTGARD-LOKI BLEW ITS STACK, CRACKING THE OUTER FACADE OF ICE.
GREAT SHEETS-- THIRTY ELLS THICK-- SLID DOWN TOWARDS US.
WHADIDYA DO?
I THINK THIS ALE WAS CURSED!
ONLY THING WE COULD. RAN! BUT TOWARDS THE ICEFALL... AND INTO THE LABYRINTH OF LOST SOULS!
ICED IN, OUR ONLY CHANCE WAS TO FORGE ON, DEEPER INTO THE TUNNELS. TWENTY DAYS WE WANDERED. LOST. GOING AROUND IN CIRCLES.
THEN, ALMOST DELIRIOUS THROUGH LACK OF FOOD, I SMELLED SULFUR. THEN FOLLOWED THE NATURAL VENT, ALL THE WAY UP TO THE JOTUN HOT SPRINGS.
FRESH AIR...
...NEVER TASTED SO GOOD.
ZZZZZ

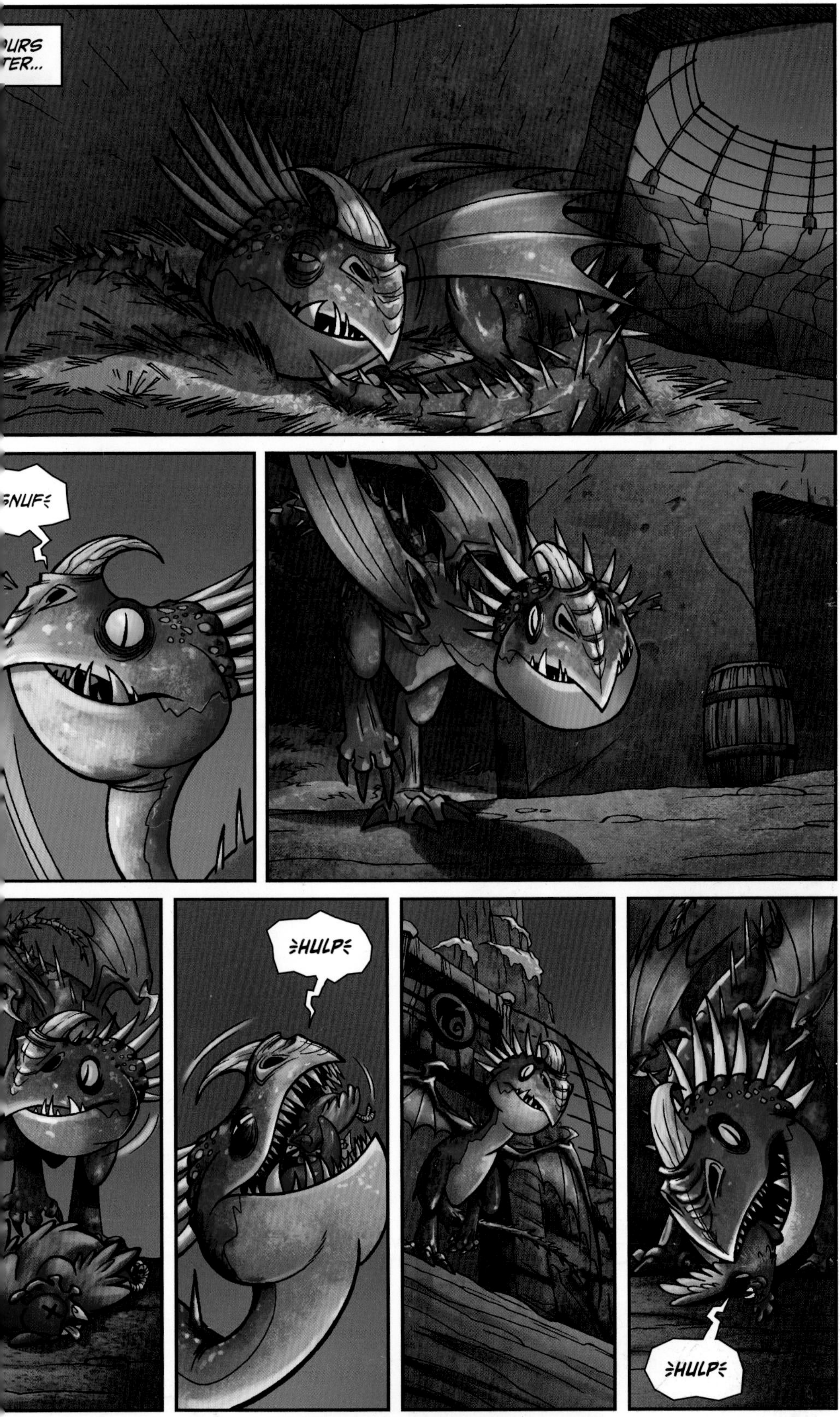
OURS
TER...
SNUF
HULP
HULP

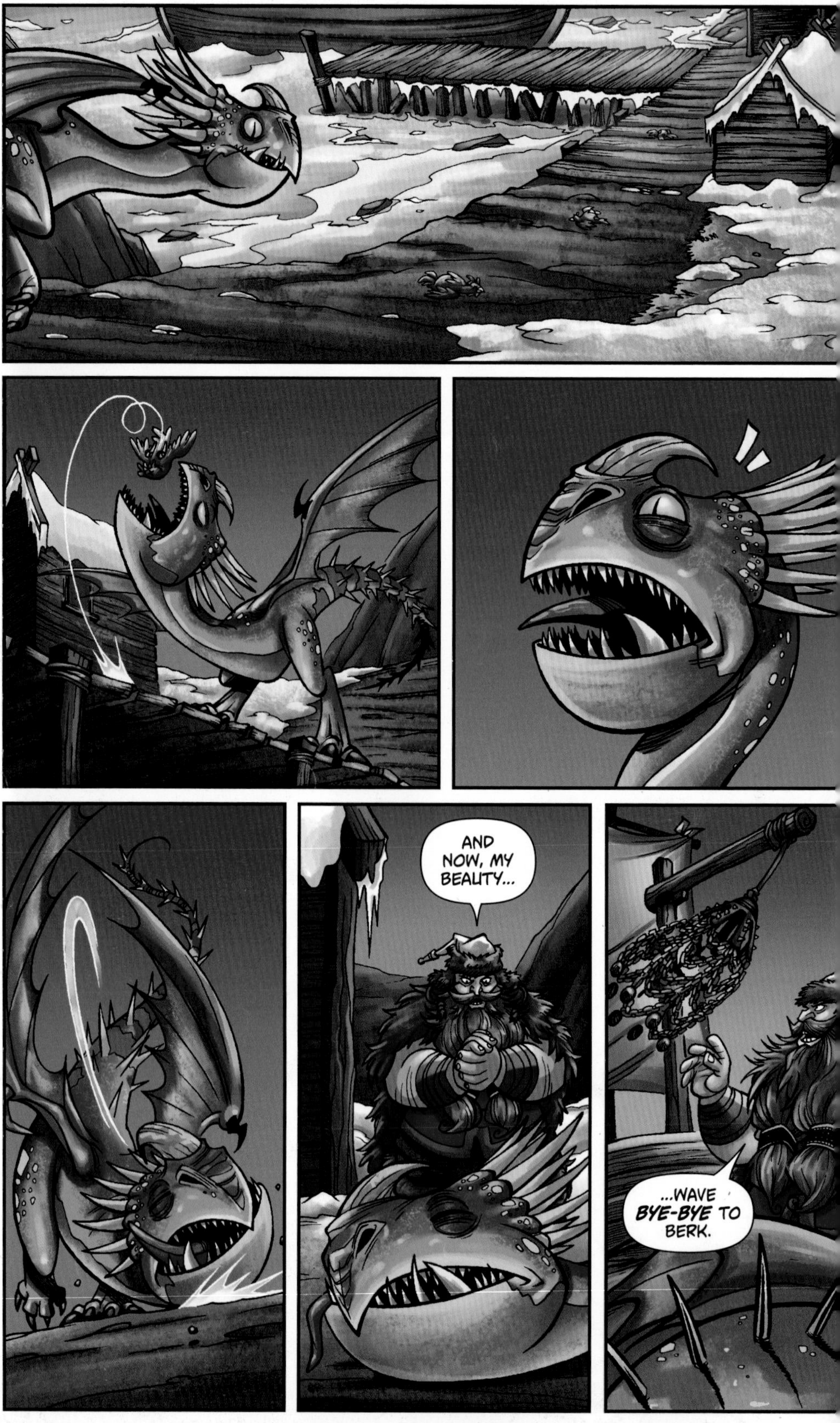
AND NOW, MY BEAUTY...
...WAVE BYE-BYE TO BERK.

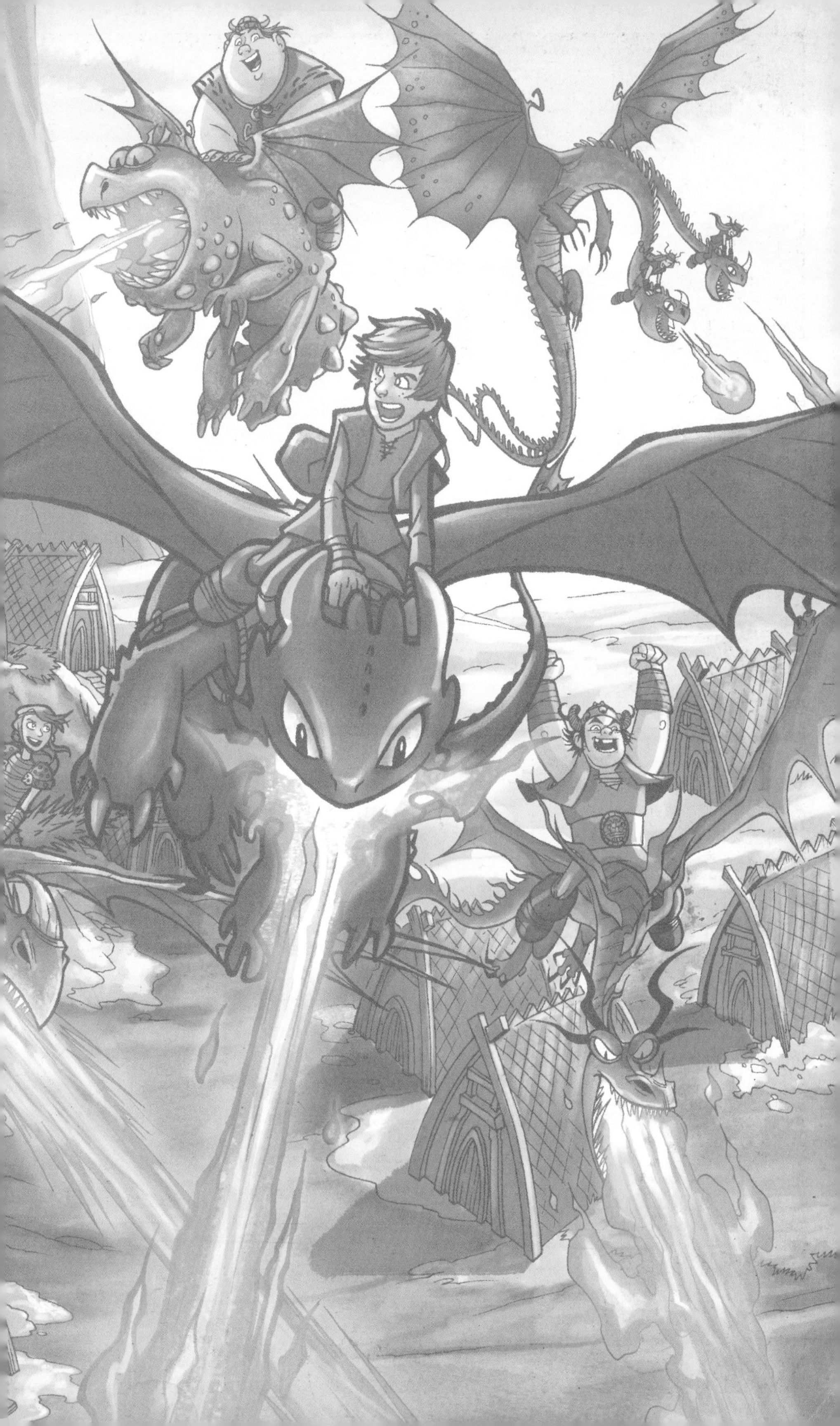

CHAPTER TWO

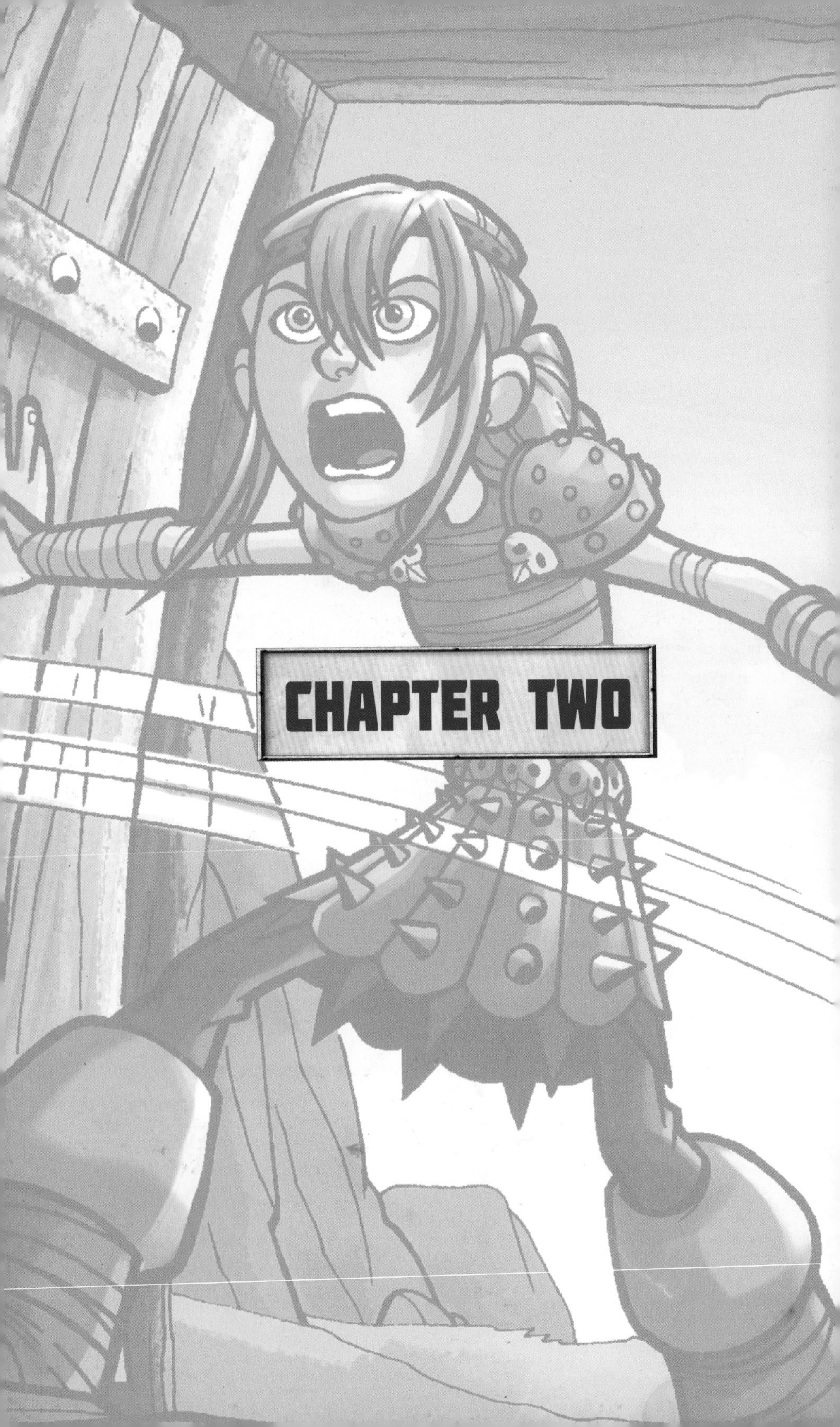

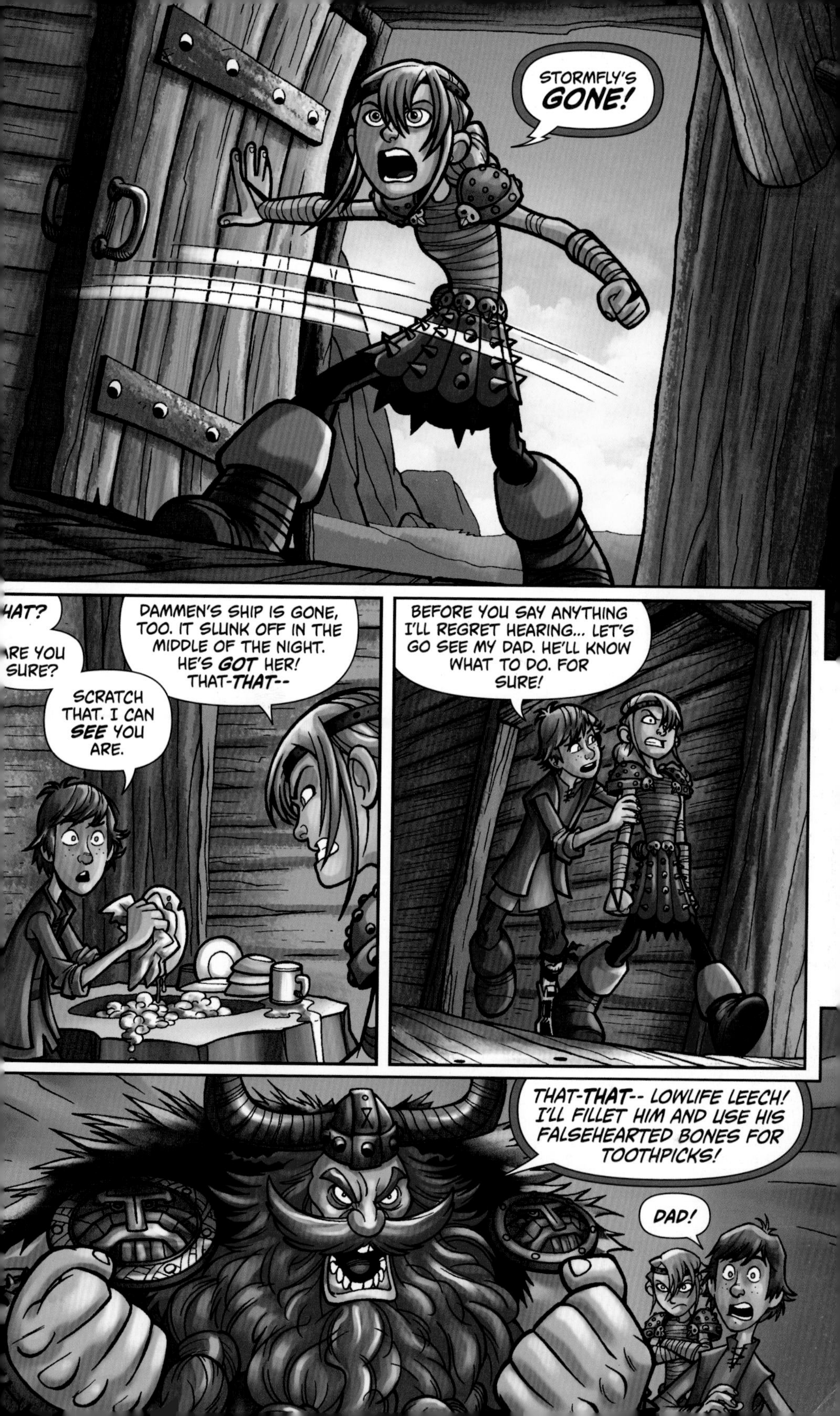
STORMFLY'S GONE!
...HAT?
...RE YOU SURE?
SCRATCH THAT. I CAN SEE YOU ARE.
DAMMEN'S SHIP IS GONE, TOO. IT SLUNK OFF IN THE MIDDLE OF THE NIGHT. HE'S GOT HER! THAT-THAT--
BEFORE YOU SAY ANYTHING I'LL REGRET HEARING... LET'S GO SEE MY DAD. HE'LL KNOW WHAT TO DO. FOR SURE!
THAT-THAT-- LOWLIFE LEECH! I'LL FILLET HIM AND USE HIS FALSEHEARTED BONES FOR TOOTHPICKS!
DAD!

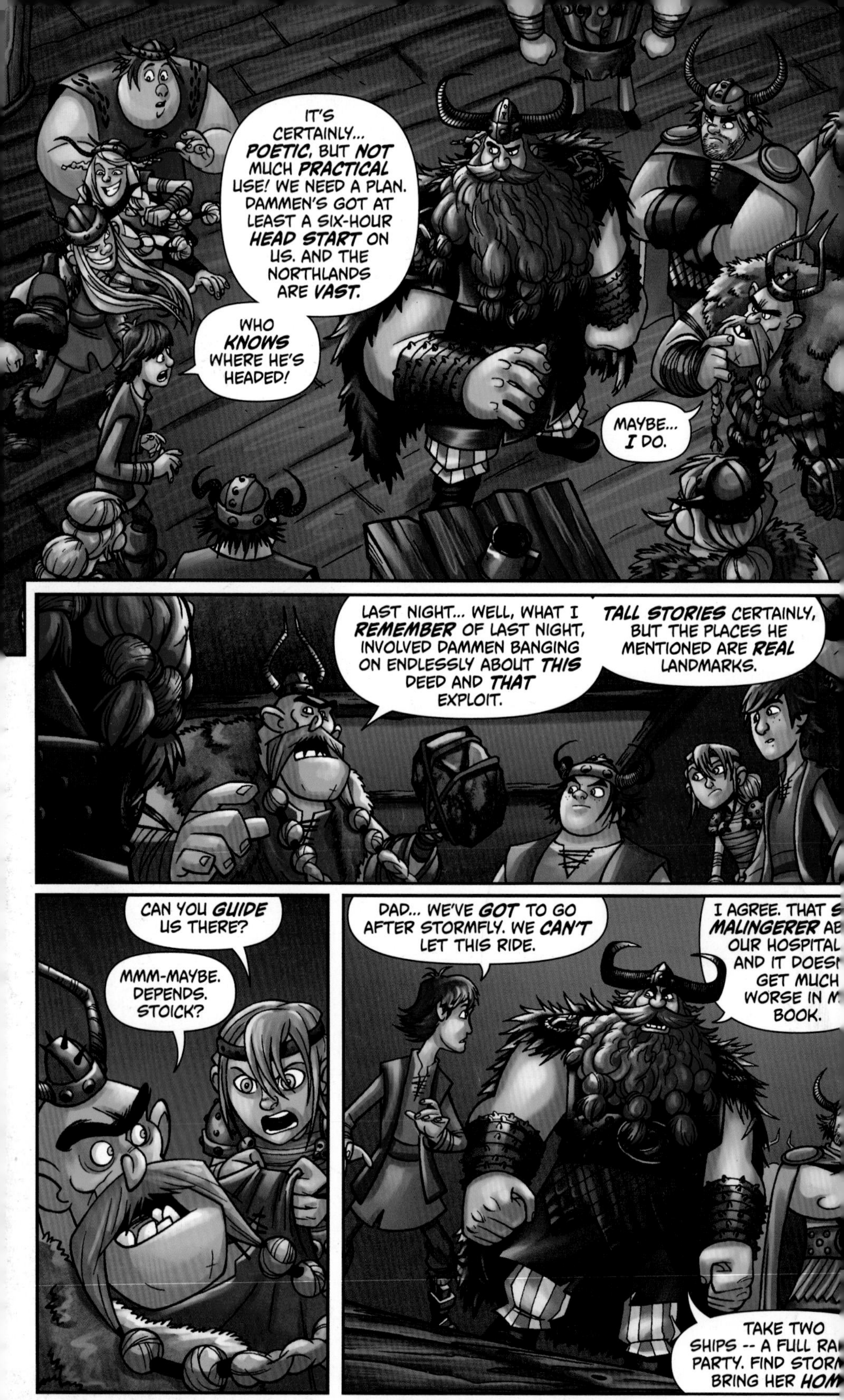
IT'S CERTAINLY... POETIC, BUT NOT MUCH PRACTICAL USE! WE NEED A PLAN. DAMMEN'S GOT AT LEAST A SIX-HOUR HEAD START ON US. AND THE NORTHLANDS ARE VAST.
WHO KNOWS WHERE HE'S HEADED!
MAYBE... I DO.
LAST NIGHT... WELL, WHAT I REMEMBER OF LAST NIGHT, INVOLVED DAMMEN BANGING ON ENDLESSLY ABOUT THIS DEED AND THAT EXPLOIT.
TALL STORIES CERTAINLY, BUT THE PLACES HE MENTIONED ARE REAL LANDMARKS.
CAN YOU GUIDE US THERE?
MMM-MAYBE. DEPENDS. STOICK?
DAD... WE'VE GOT TO GO AFTER STORMFLY. WE CAN'T LET THIS RIDE.
I AGREE. THAT
MALINGERER
OUR HOSPITAL
AND IT DOES
GET MUCH
WORSE IN
BOOK.
TAKE TWO
SHIPS -- A FULL
PARTY. FIND
BRING HER

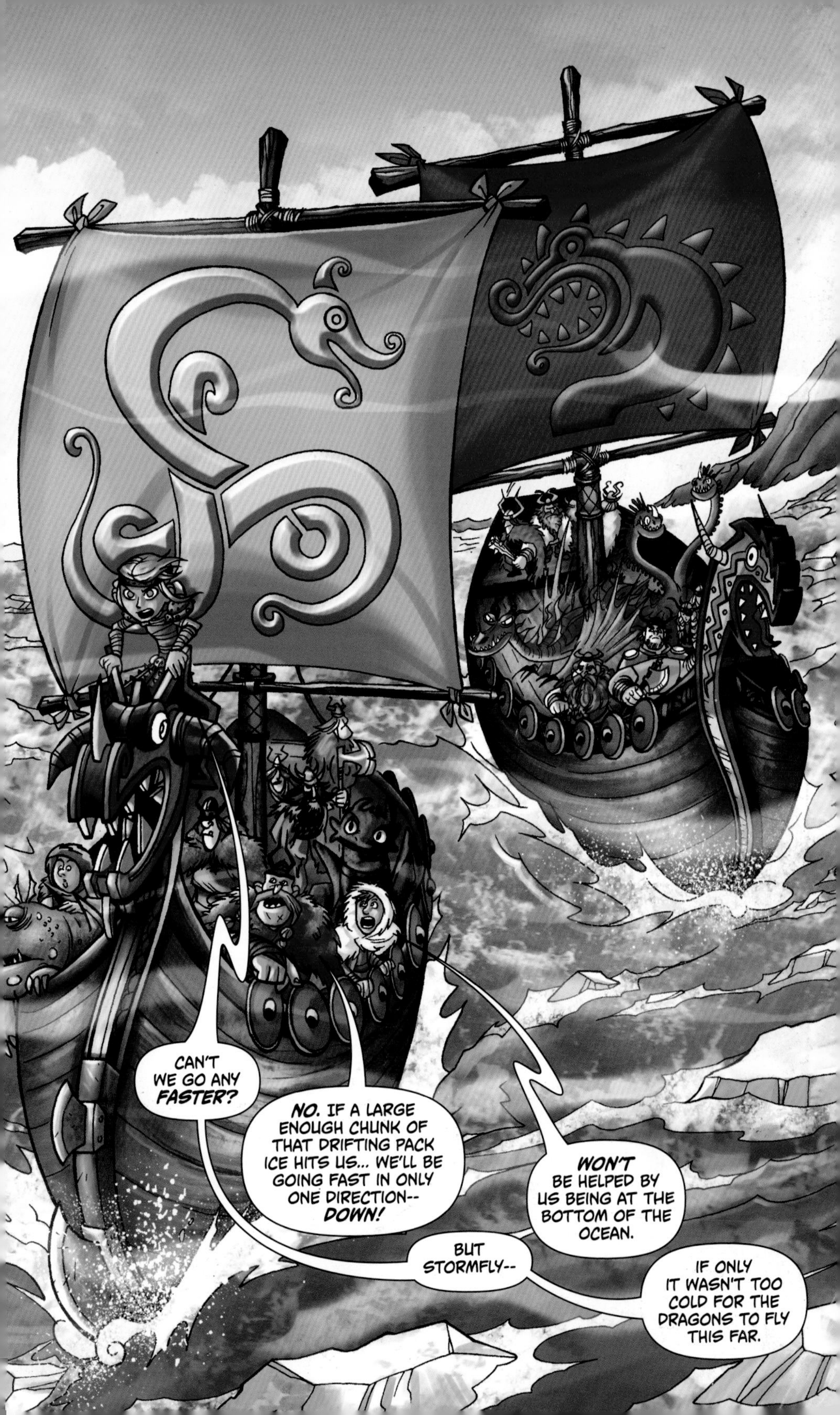

CAN'T WE GO ANY *FASTER?*
NO. IF A LARGE ENOUGH CHUNK OF THAT DRIFTING PACK ICE HITS US... WE'LL BE GOING FAST IN ONLY ONE DIRECTION-- *DOWN!*
BUT STORMFLY--
WON'T BE HELPED BY US BEING AT THE BOTTOM OF THE OCEAN.
IF ONLY IT WASN'T TOO COLD FOR THE DRAGONS TO FLY THIS FAR.

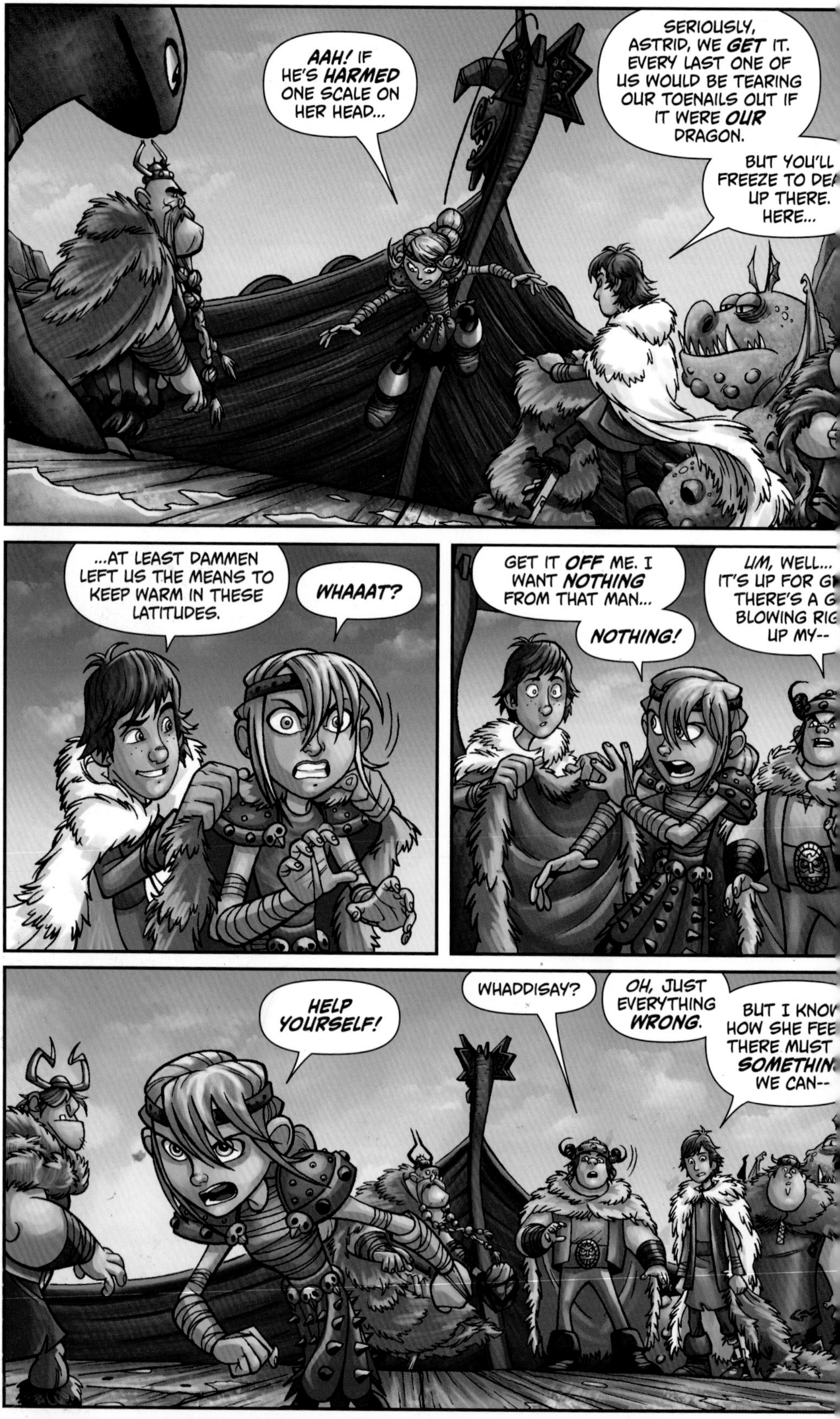
AAH! IF HE'S HARMED ONE SCALE ON HER HEAD...
SERIOUSLY, ASTRID, WE GET IT. EVERY LAST ONE OF US WOULD BE TEARING OUR TOENAILS OUT IF IT WERE OUR DRAGON.
BUT YOU'LL FREEZE TO DE UP THERE. HERE...
...AT LEAST DAMMEN LEFT US THE MEANS TO KEEP WARM IN THESE LATITUDES.
WHAAAT?
GET IT OFF ME. I WANT NOTHING FROM THAT MAN...
NOTHING!
UM, WELL... IT'S UP FOR G THERE'S A G BLOWING RIG UP MY--
HELP YOURSELF!
WHADDISAY?
OH, JUST EVERYTHING WRONG.
BUT I KNOV HOW SHE FEE THERE MUST SOMETHIN WE CAN--

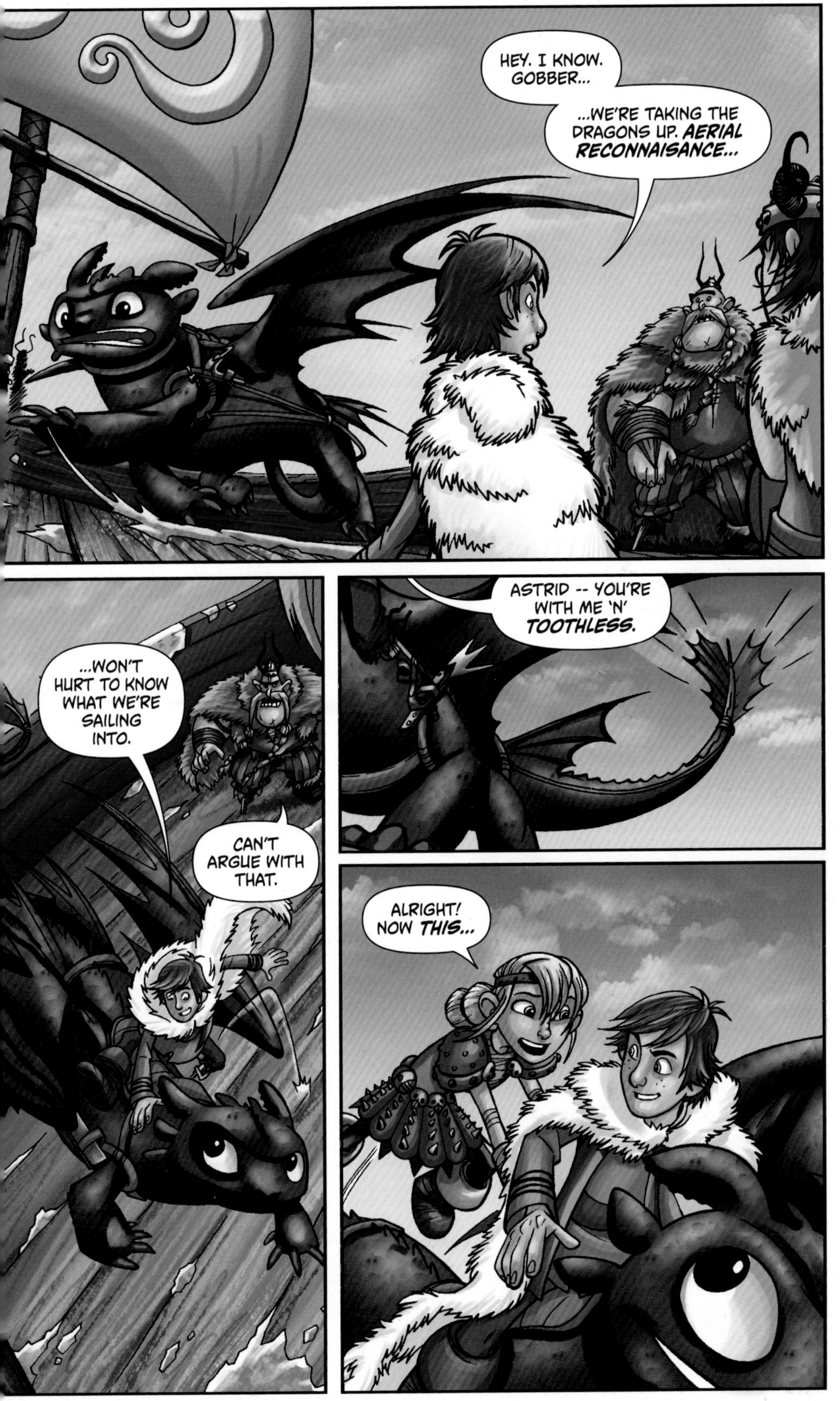

HEY. I KNOW. GOBBER...
...WE'RE TAKING THE DRAGONS UP. AERIAL RECONNAISANCE...
...WON'T HURT TO KNOW WHAT WE'RE SAILING INTO.
CAN'T ARGUE WITH THAT.
ASTRID -- YOU'RE WITH ME 'N' TOOTHLESS.
ALRIGHT! NOW THIS...

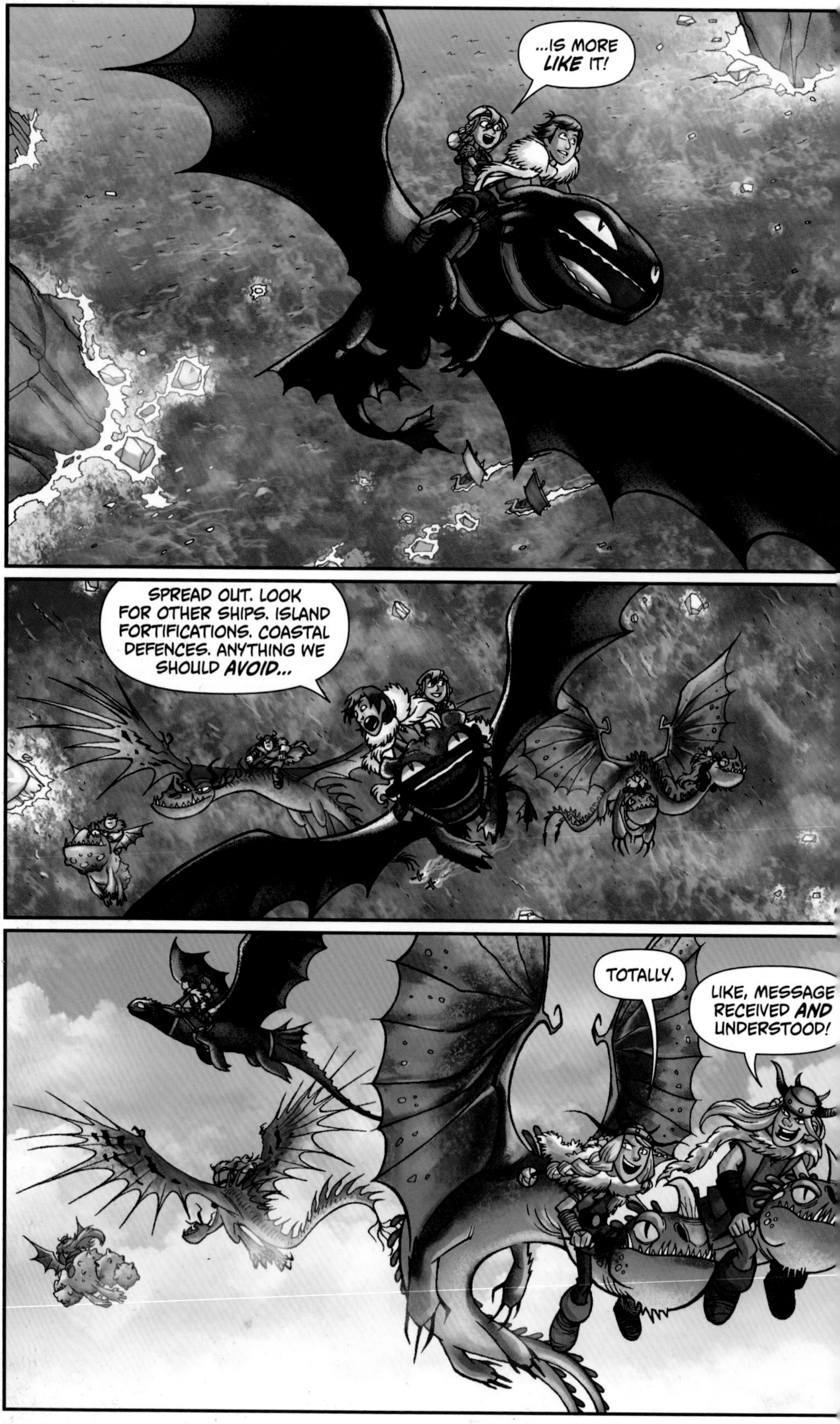
...IS MORE LIKE IT!
SPREAD OUT. LOOK FOR OTHER SHIPS. ISLAND FORTIFICATIONS. COASTAL DEFENCES. ANYTHING WE SHOULD AVOID...
TOTALLY.
LIKE, MESSAGE RECEIVED AND UNDERSTOOD!

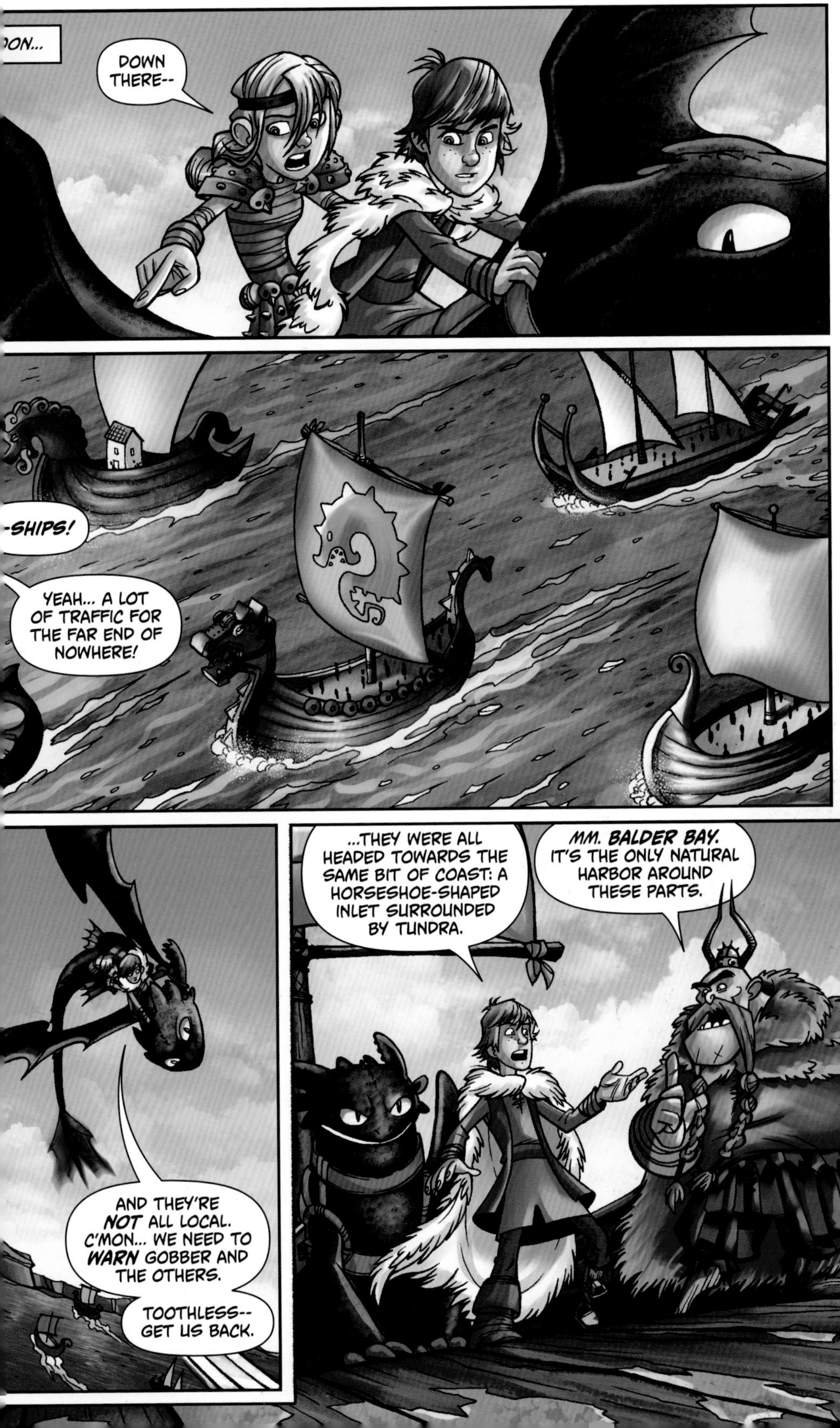

...ON...
DOWN THERE--
-SHIPS!
YEAH... A LOT OF TRAFFIC FOR THE FAR END OF NOWHERE!
AND THEY'RE NOT ALL LOCAL. C'MON... WE NEED TO WARN GOBBER AND THE OTHERS.
TOOTHLESS-- GET US BACK.
...THEY WERE ALL HEADED TOWARDS THE SAME BIT OF COAST: A HORSESHOE-SHAPED INLET SURROUNDED BY TUNDRA.
MM. BALDER BAY. IT'S THE ONLY NATURAL HARBOR AROUND THESE PARTS.

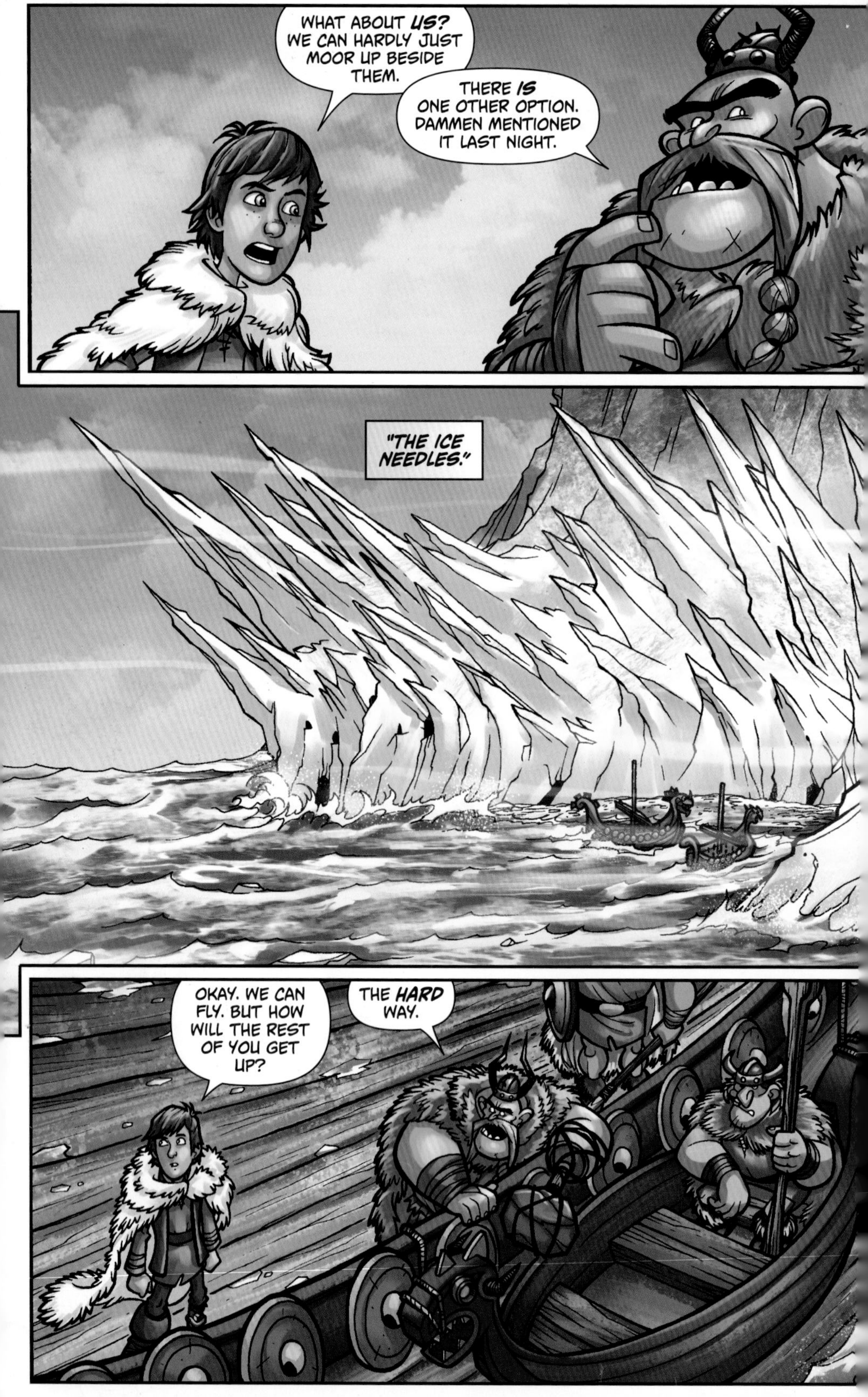
WHAT ABOUT US? WE CAN HARDLY JUST MOOR UP BESIDE THEM.
THERE IS ONE OTHER OPTION. DAMMEN MENTIONED IT LAST NIGHT.
"THE ICE NEEDLES."
OKAY. WE CAN FLY. BUT HOW WILL THE REST OF YOU GET UP?
THE HARD WAY.

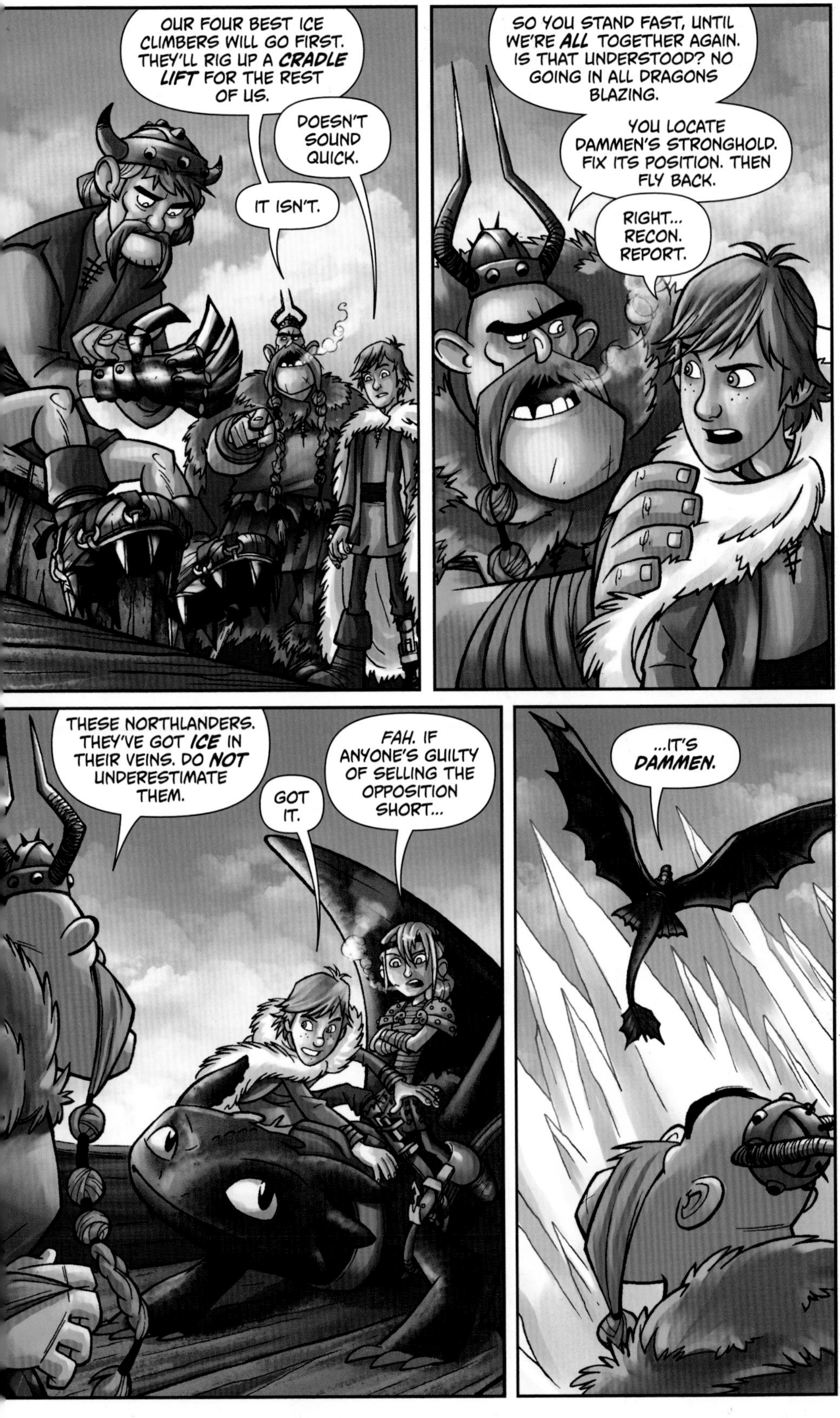
OUR FOUR BEST ICE CLIMBERS WILL GO FIRST. THEY'LL RIG UP A *CRADLE LIFT* FOR THE REST OF US.
DOESN'T SOUND QUICK.
IT ISN'T.
SO YOU STAND FAST, UNTIL WE'RE *ALL* TOGETHER AGAIN. IS THAT UNDERSTOOD? NO GOING IN ALL DRAGONS BLAZING.
YOU LOCATE DAMMEN'S STRONGHOLD. FIX ITS POSITION. THEN FLY BACK.
RIGHT... RECON. REPORT.
THESE NORTHLANDERS. THEY'VE GOT *ICE* IN THEIR VEINS. DO *NOT* UNDERESTIMATE THEM.
GOT IT.
FAH. IF ANYONE'S GUILTY OF SELLING THE OPPOSITION SHORT...
...IT'S *DAMMEN*.

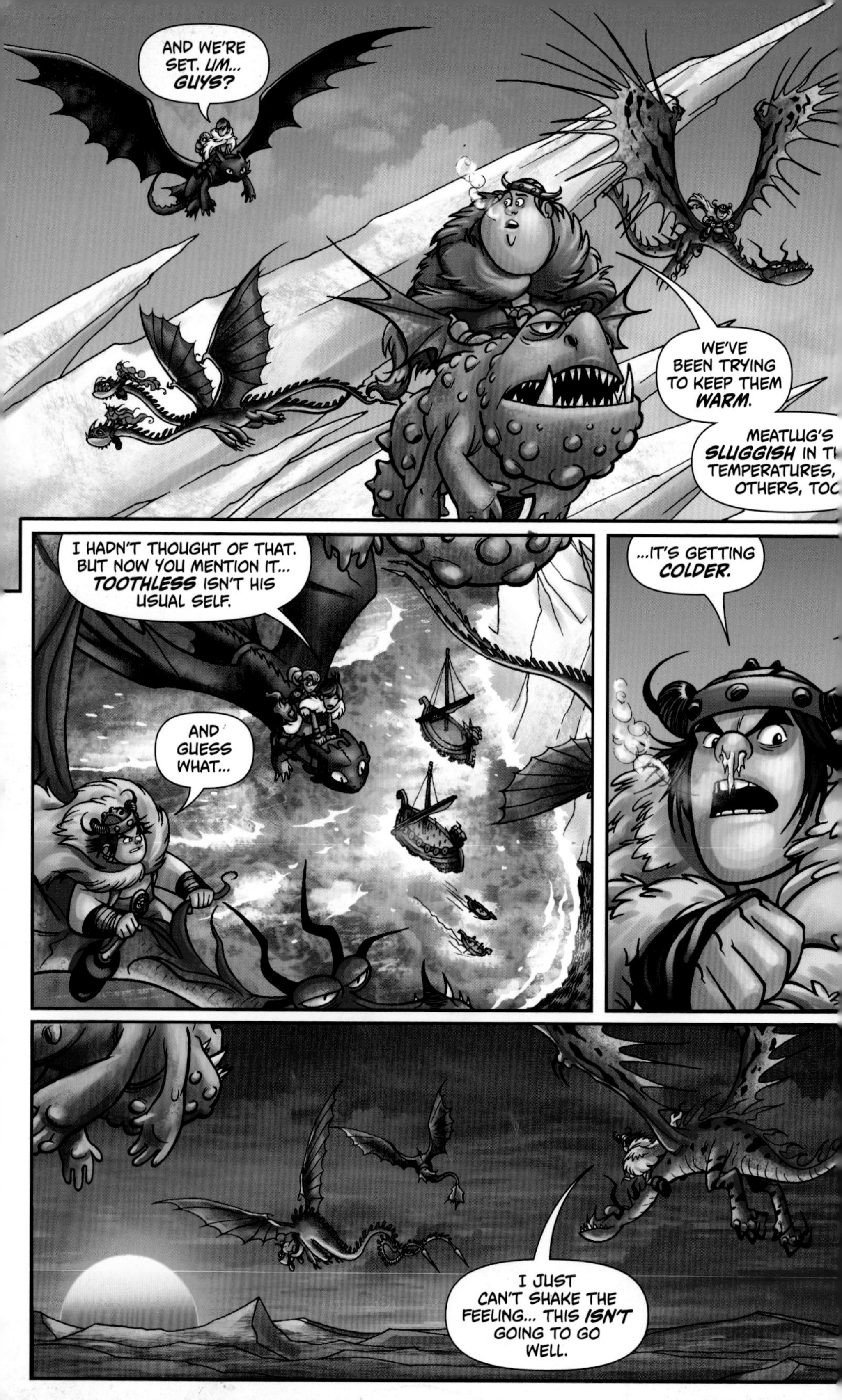
AND WE'RE SET. UM... GUYS?
WE'VE BEEN TRYING TO KEEP THEM WARM.
MEATLUG'S SLUGGISH IN T TEMPERATURES, OTHERS, TOO
I HADN'T THOUGHT OF THAT. BUT NOW YOU MENTION IT... TOOTHLESS ISN'T HIS USUAL SELF.
AND GUESS WHAT...
...IT'S GETTING COLDER.
I JUST CAN'T SHAKE THE FEELING... THIS ISN'T GOING TO GO WELL.

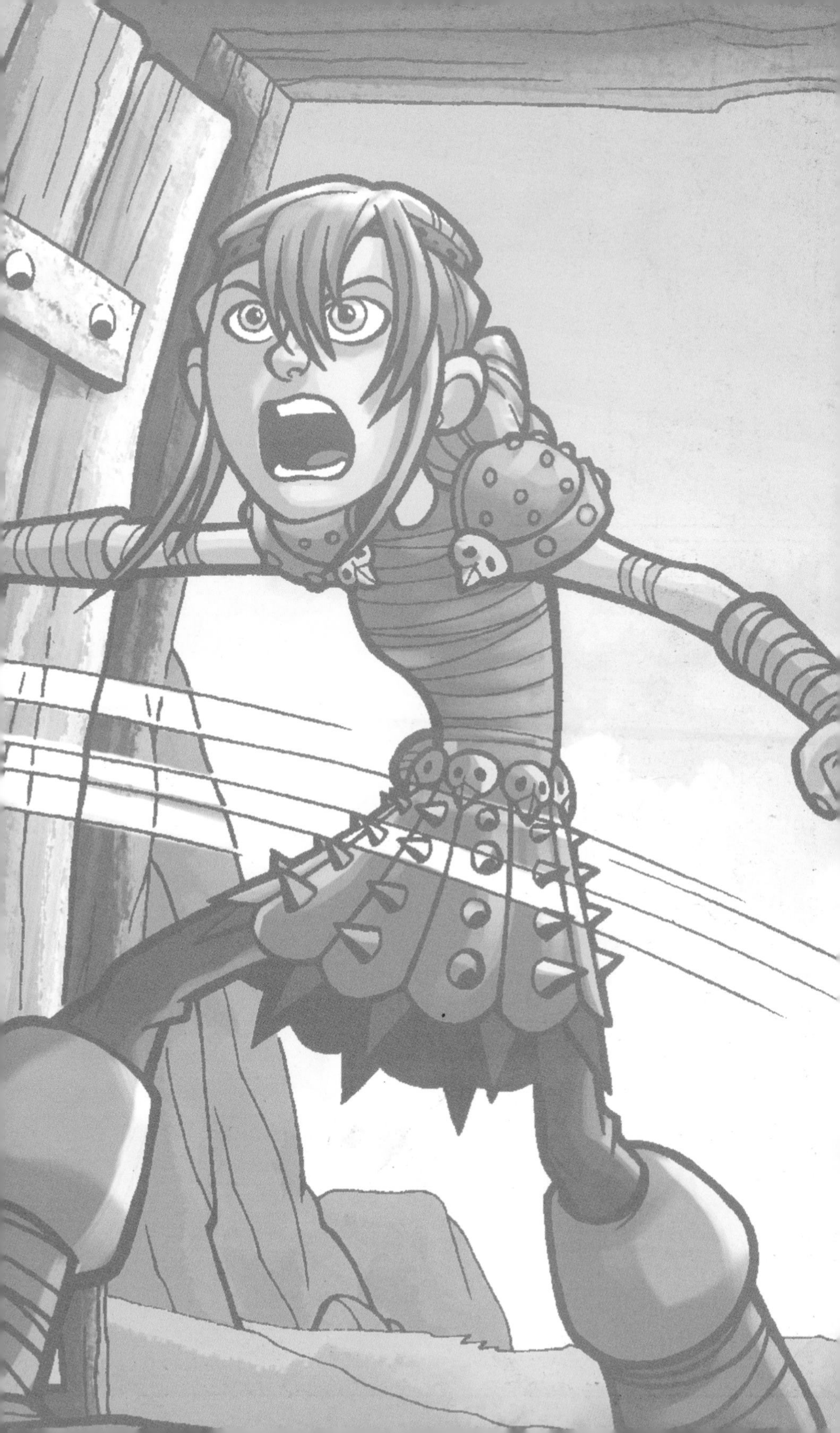

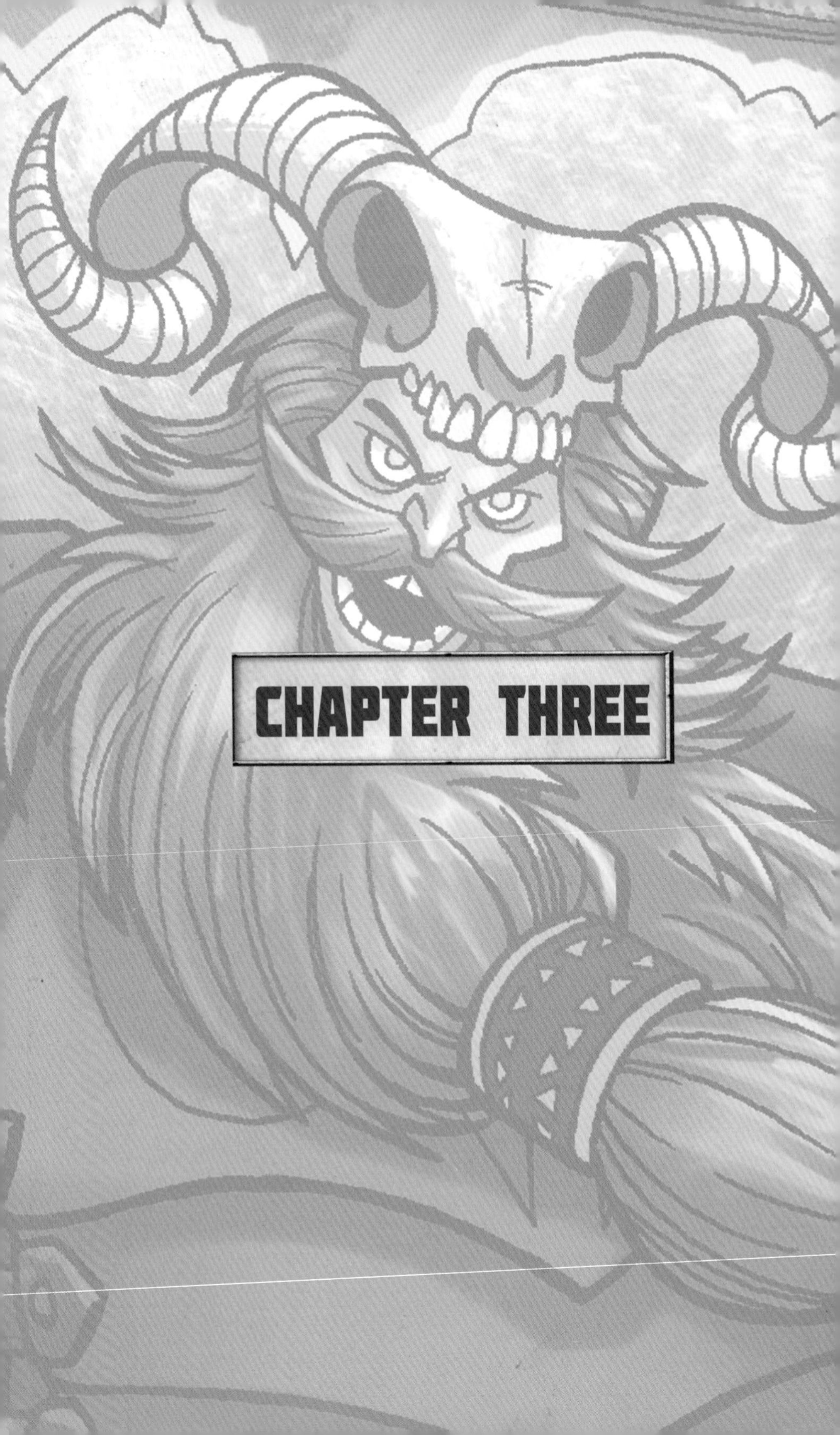

CHAPTER THREE

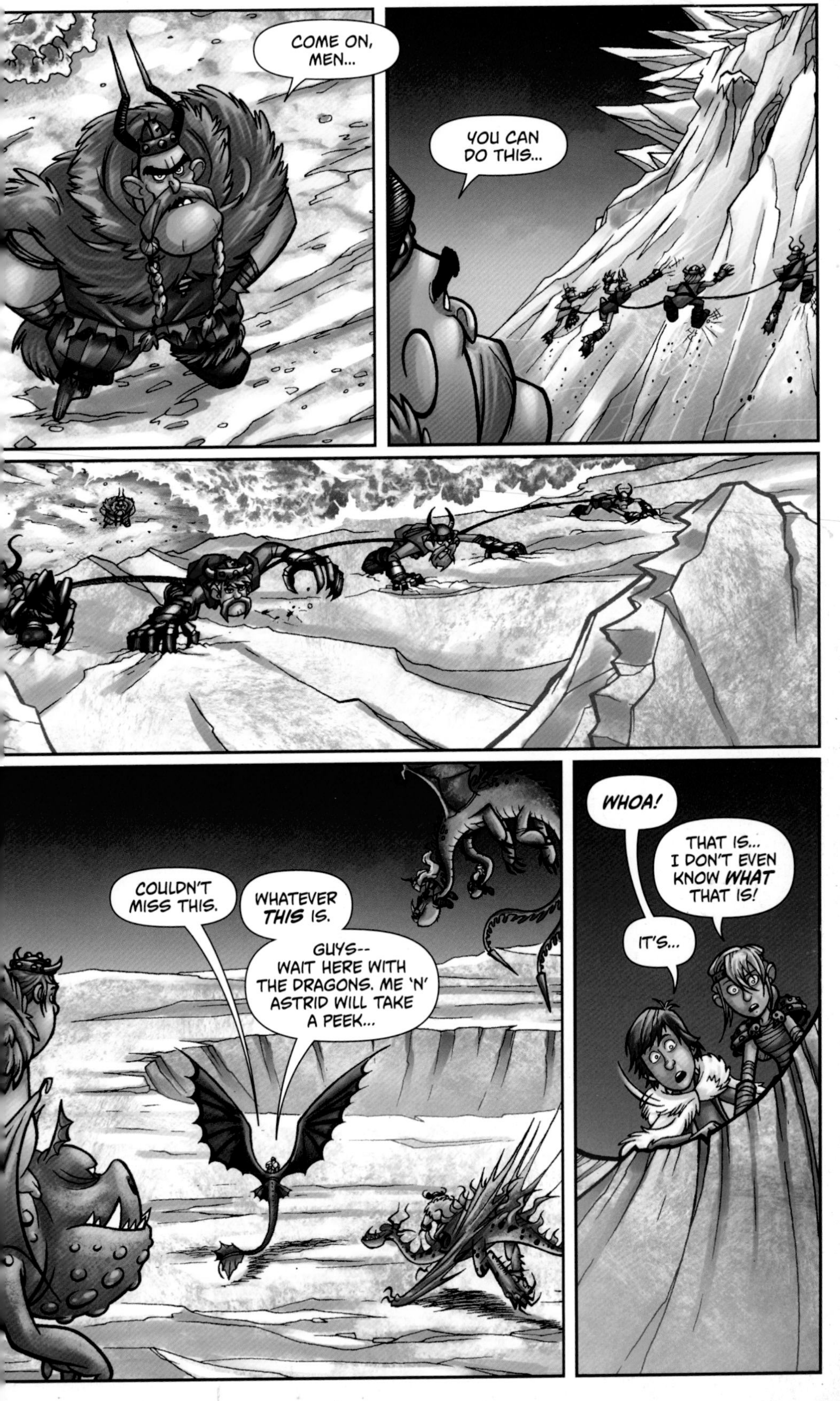
COME ON, MEN...
YOU CAN DO THIS...
COULDN'T MISS THIS.
WHATEVER *THIS* IS.
GUYS-- WAIT HERE WITH THE DRAGONS. ME 'N' ASTRID WILL TAKE A PEEK...
WHOA!
THAT IS... I DON'T EVEN KNOW *WHAT* THAT IS!
IT'S...

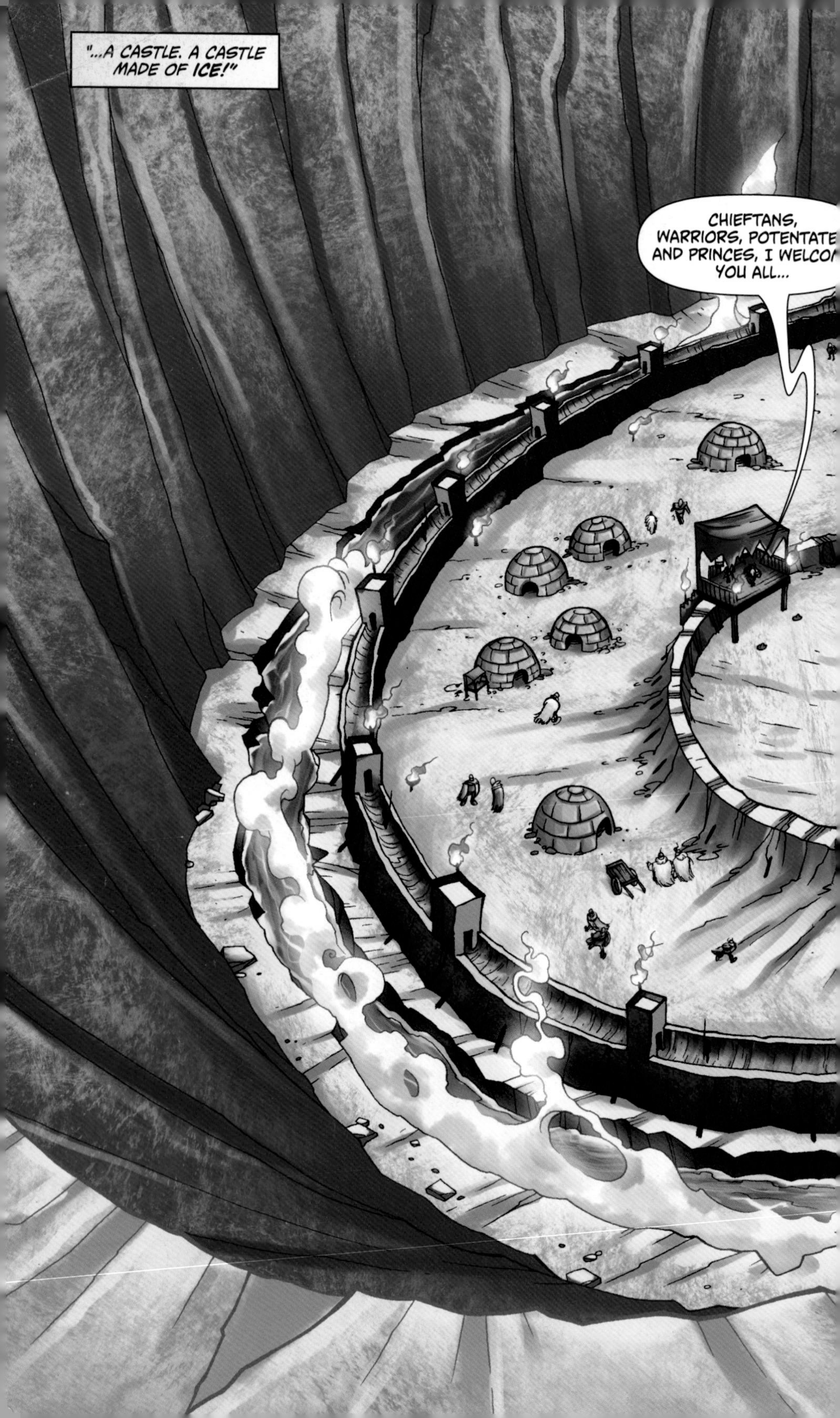
"...A CASTLE. A CASTLE MADE OF ICE!"
CHIEFTANS, WARRIORS, POTENTATE AND PRINCES, I WELCOM YOU ALL...

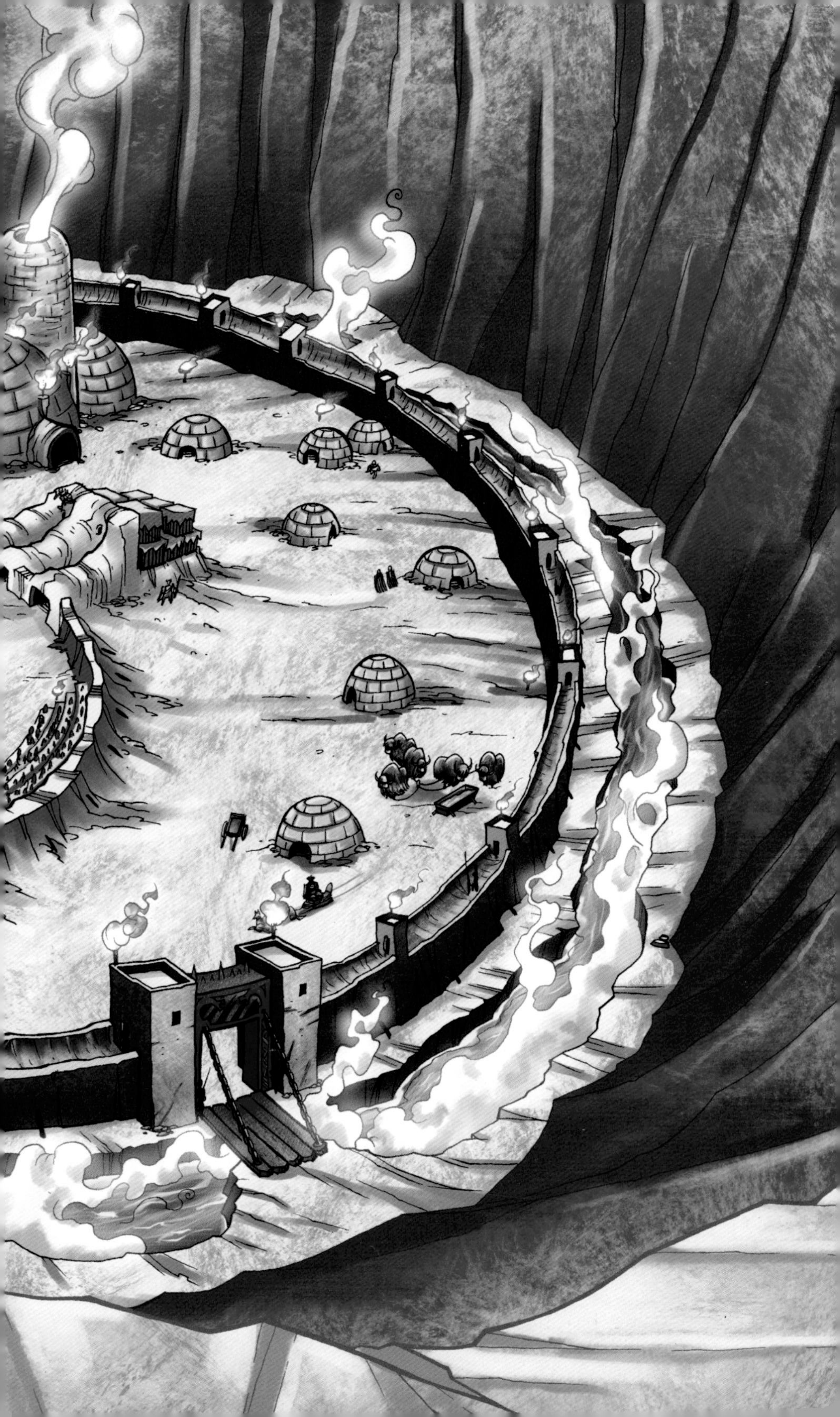

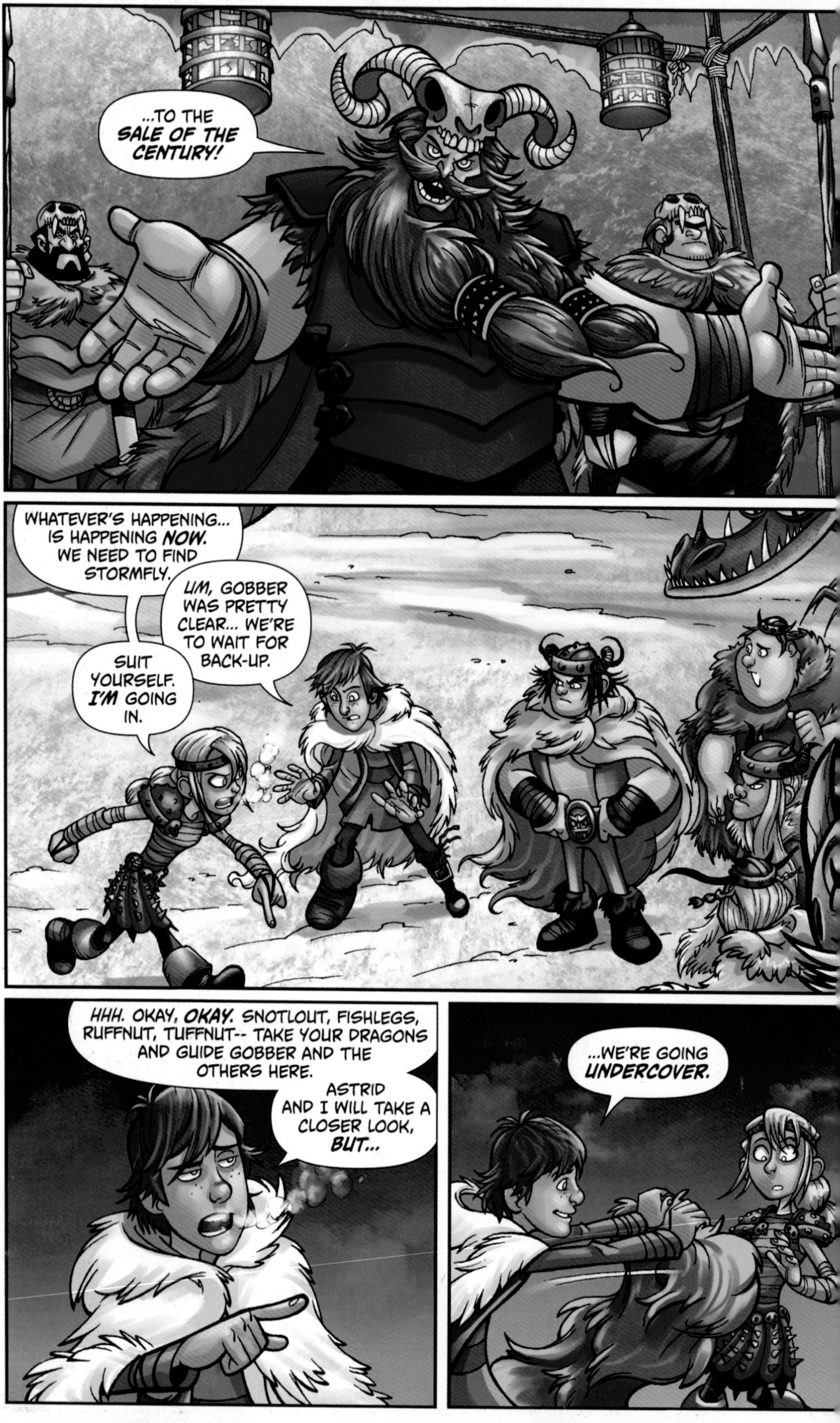
...TO THE SALE OF THE CENTURY!
WHATEVER'S HAPPENING... IS HAPPENING NOW. WE NEED TO FIND STORMFLY.
UM, GOBBER WAS PRETTY CLEAR... WE'RE TO WAIT FOR BACK-UP.
SUIT YOURSELF. I'M GOING IN.
HHH. OKAY, OKAY. SNOTLOUT, FISHLEGS, RUFFNUT, TUFFNUT-- TAKE YOUR DRAGONS AND GUIDE GOBBER AND THE OTHERS HERE.
ASTRID AND I WILL TAKE A CLOSER LOOK, BUT...
...WE'RE GOING UNDERCOVER.

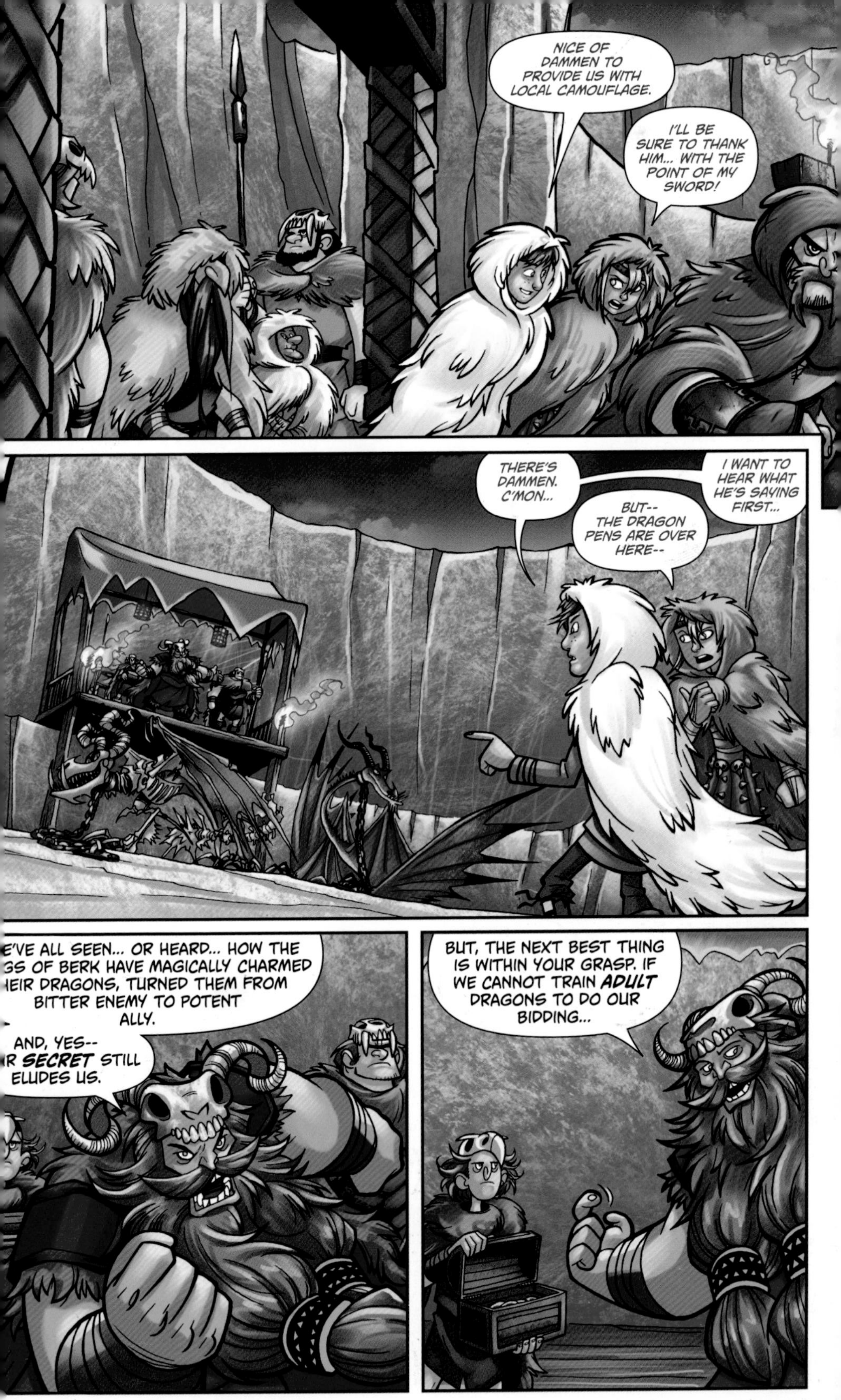
NICE OF DAMMEN TO PROVIDE US WITH LOCAL CAMOUFLAGE.
I'LL BE SURE TO THANK HIM... WITH THE POINT OF MY SWORD!
THERE'S DAMMEN. C'MON...
BUT-- THE DRAGON PENS ARE OVER HERE--
I WANT TO HEAR WHAT HE'S SAYING FIRST...
E'VE ALL SEEN... OR HEARD... HOW THE GS OF BERK HAVE MAGICALLY CHARMED HEIR DRAGONS, TURNED THEM FROM BITTER ENEMY TO POTENT ALLY.
AND, YES-- R SECRET STILL ELUDES US.
BUT, THE NEXT BEST THING IS WITHIN YOUR GRASP. IF WE CANNOT TRAIN ADULT DRAGONS TO DO OUR BIDDING...

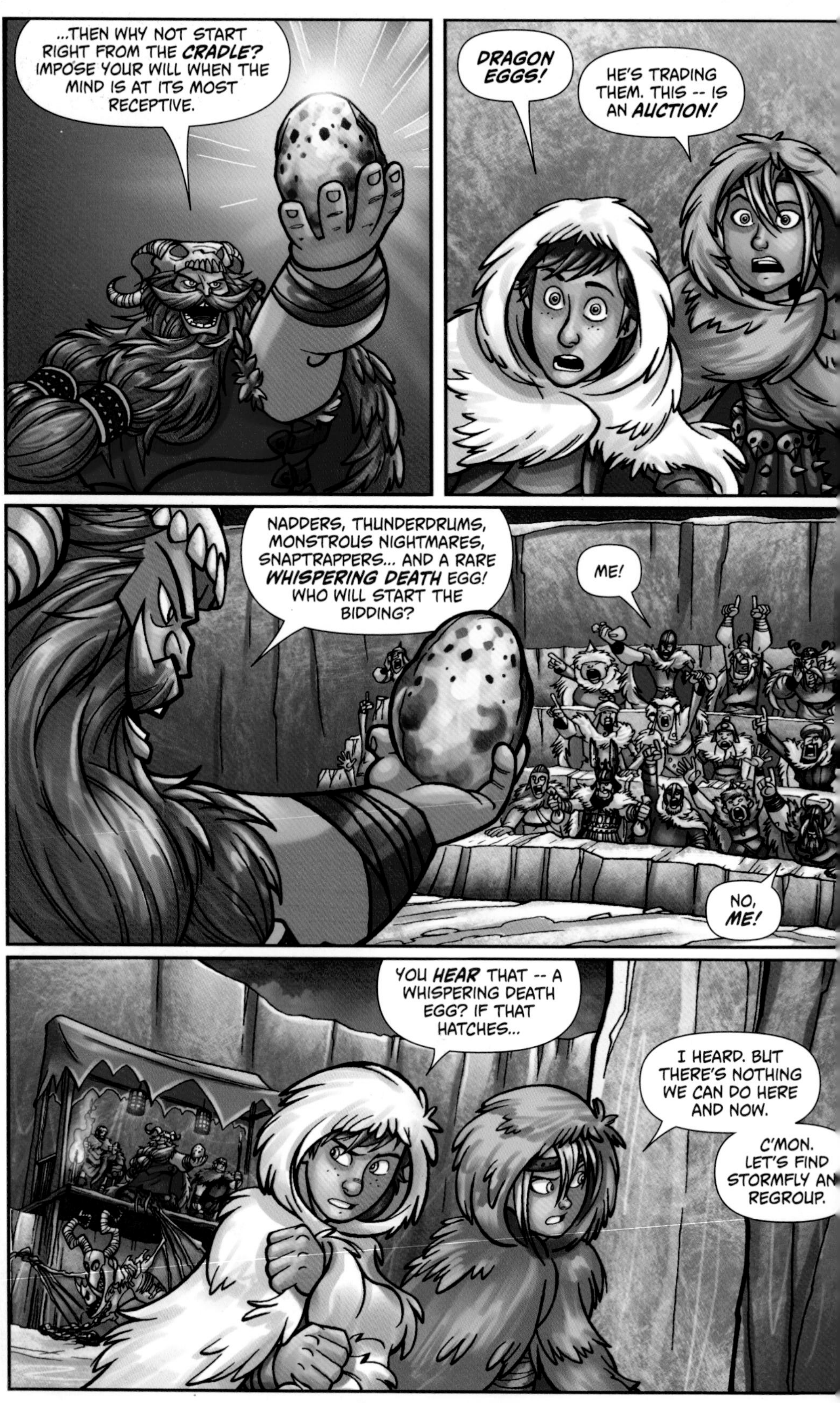
...THEN WHY NOT START RIGHT FROM THE CRADLE? IMPOSE YOUR WILL WHEN THE MIND IS AT ITS MOST RECEPTIVE.
DRAGON EGGS!
HE'S TRADING THEM. THIS -- IS AN AUCTION!
NADDERS, THUNDERDRUMS, MONSTROUS NIGHTMARES, SNAPTRAPPERS... AND A RARE WHISPERING DEATH EGG! WHO WILL START THE BIDDING?
ME!
NO, ME!
YOU HEAR THAT -- A WHISPERING DEATH EGG? IF THAT HATCHES...
I HEARD. BUT THERE'S NOTHING WE CAN DO HERE AND NOW.
C'MON. LET'S FIND STORMFLY AN REGROUP.

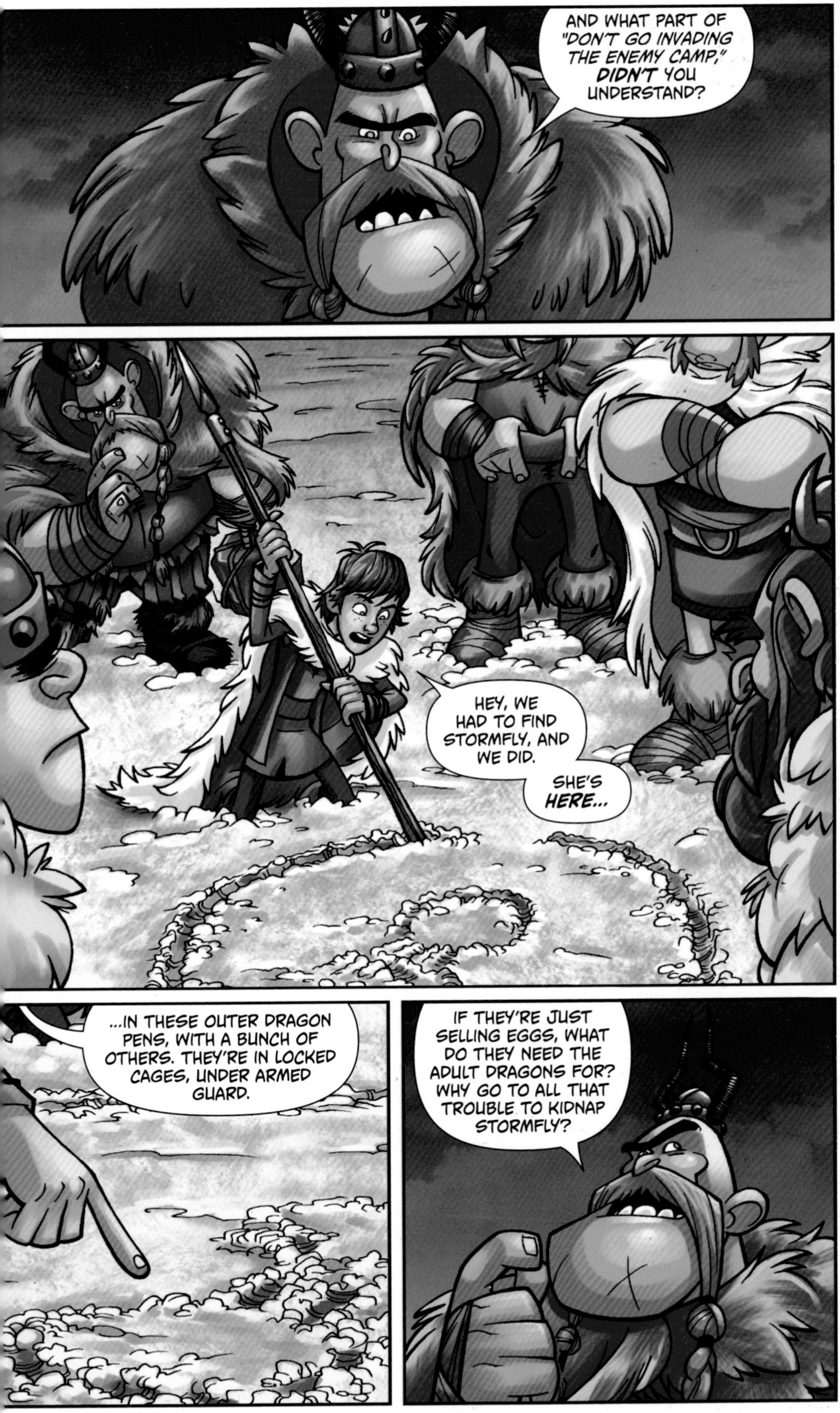
AND WHAT PART OF "DON'T GO INVADING THE ENEMY CAMP," DIDN'T YOU UNDERSTAND?
HEY, WE HAD TO FIND STORMFLY, AND WE DID.
SHE'S HERE...
...IN THESE OUTER DRAGON PENS, WITH A BUNCH OF OTHERS. THEY'RE IN LOCKED CAGES, UNDER ARMED GUARD.
IF THEY'RE JUST SELLING EGGS, WHAT DO THEY NEED THE ADULT DRAGONS FOR? WHY GO TO ALL THAT TROUBLE TO KIDNAP STORMFLY?

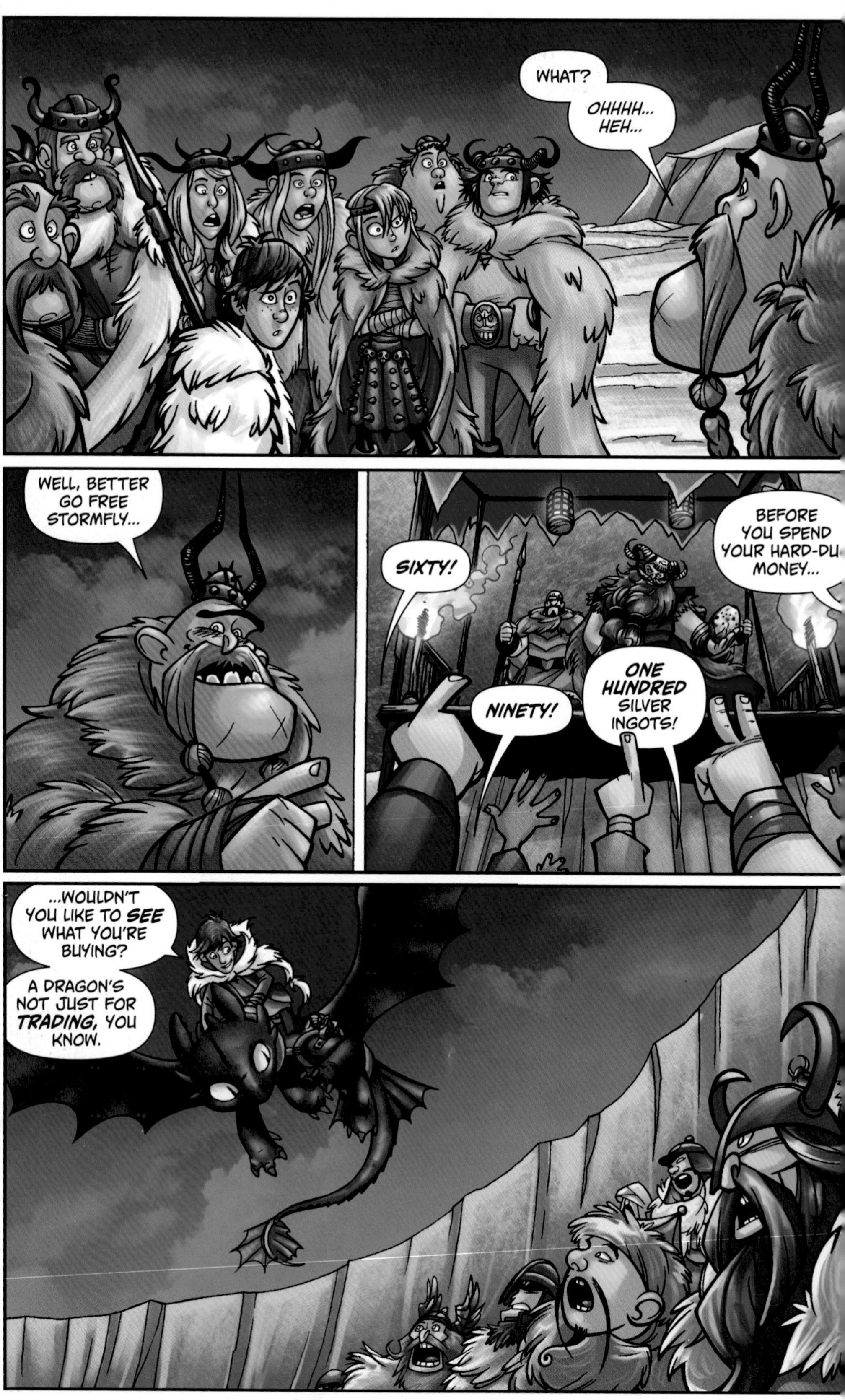
WHAT?
OHHHH... HEH...
WELL, BETTER GO FREE STORMFLY...
SIXTY!
BEFORE YOU SPEND YOUR HARD-DU MONEY...
ONE HUNDRED SILVER INGOTS!
NINETY!
...WOULDN'T YOU LIKE TO SEE WHAT YOU'RE BUYING?
A DRAGON'S NOT JUST FOR TRADING, YOU KNOW.

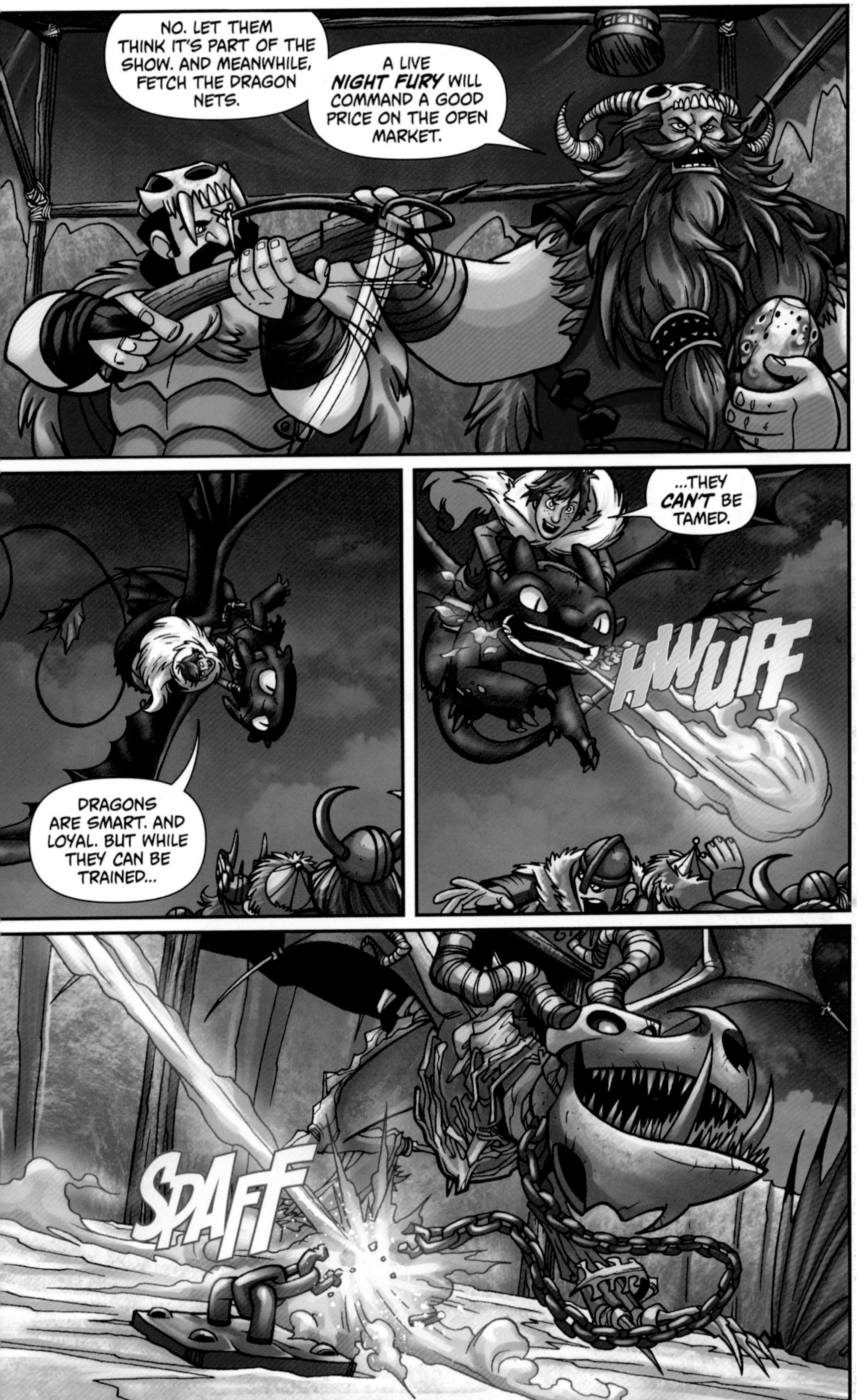
NO. LET THEM THINK IT'S PART OF THE SHOW. AND MEANWHILE, FETCH THE DRAGON NETS.
A LIVE *NIGHT FURY* WILL COMMAND A GOOD PRICE ON THE OPEN MARKET.
DRAGONS ARE SMART. AND LOYAL. BUT WHILE THEY CAN BE TRAINED...
...THEY *CAN'T* BE TAMED.
HWUFF
SPAFF

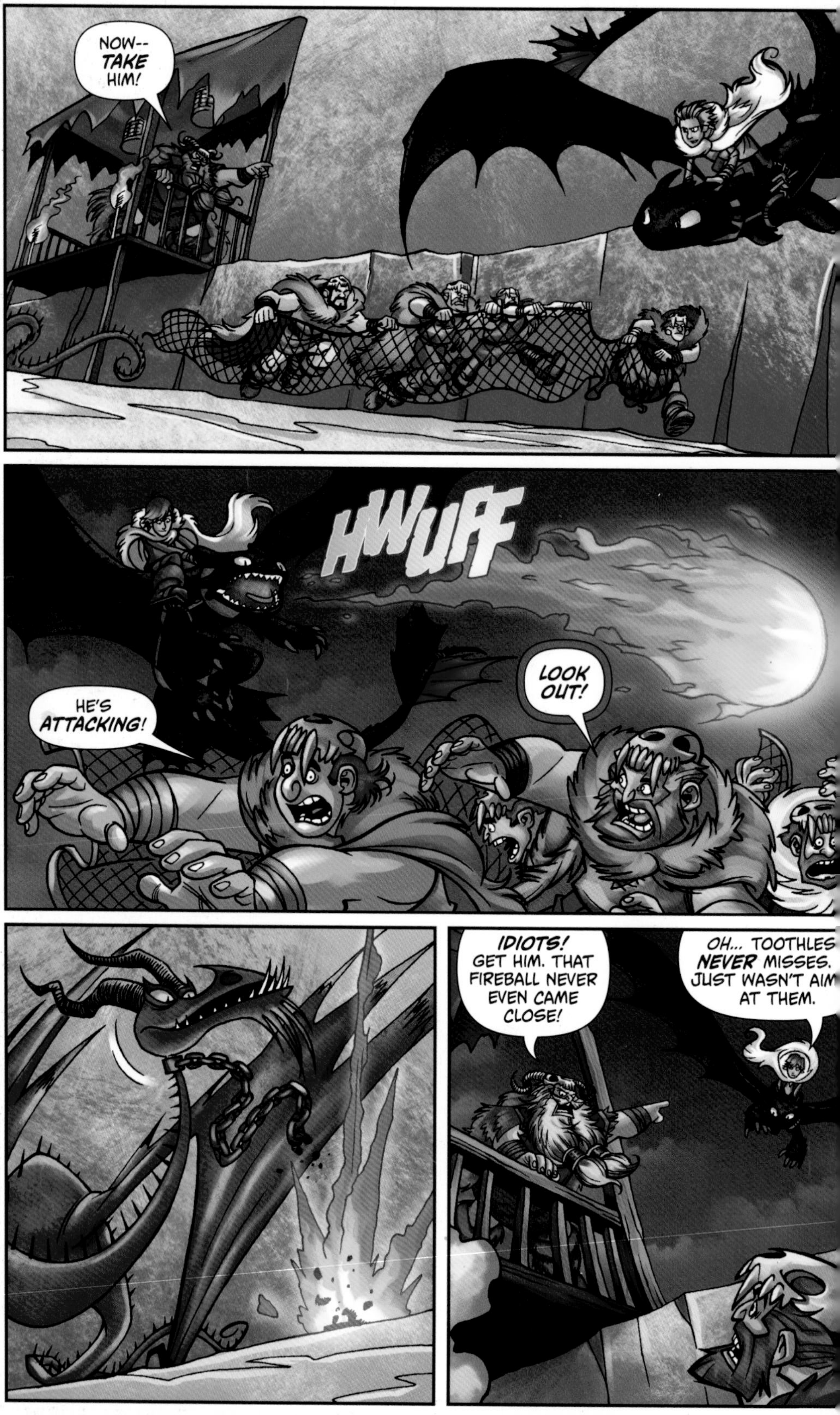
NOW-- TAKE HIM!
HWUFF
HE'S ATTACKING!
LOOK OUT!
IDIOTS! GET HIM. THAT FIREBALL NEVER EVEN CAME CLOSE!
OH... TOOTHLES NEVER MISSES. JUST WASN'T AIM AT THEM.

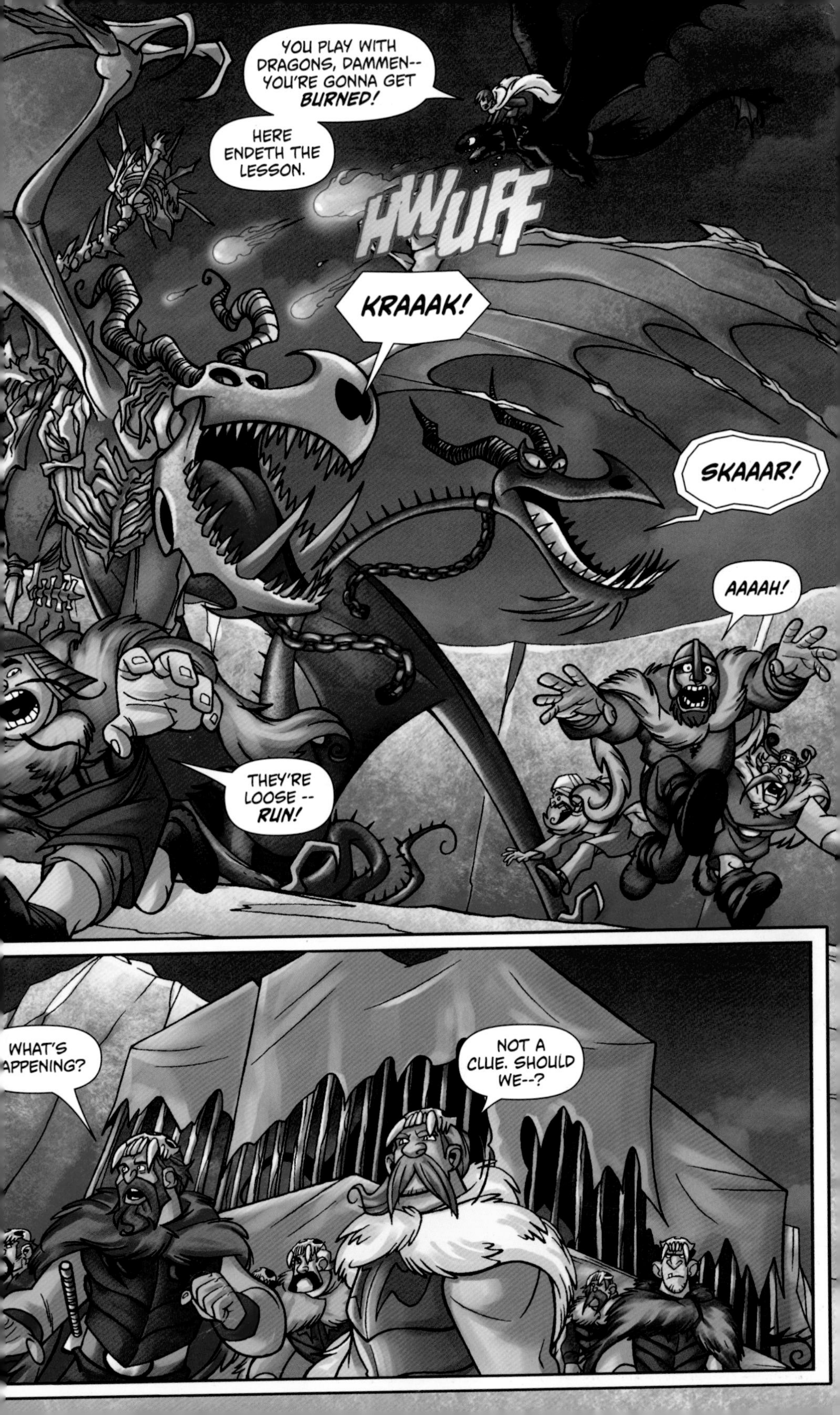
YOU PLAY WITH DRAGONS, DAMMEN-- YOU'RE GONNA GET BURNED!
HERE ENDETH THE LESSON.
HWUFF
KRAAAK!
SKAAAR!
AAAAH!
THEY'RE LOOSE -- RUN!
WHAT'S APPENING?
NOT A CLUE. SHOULD WE--?

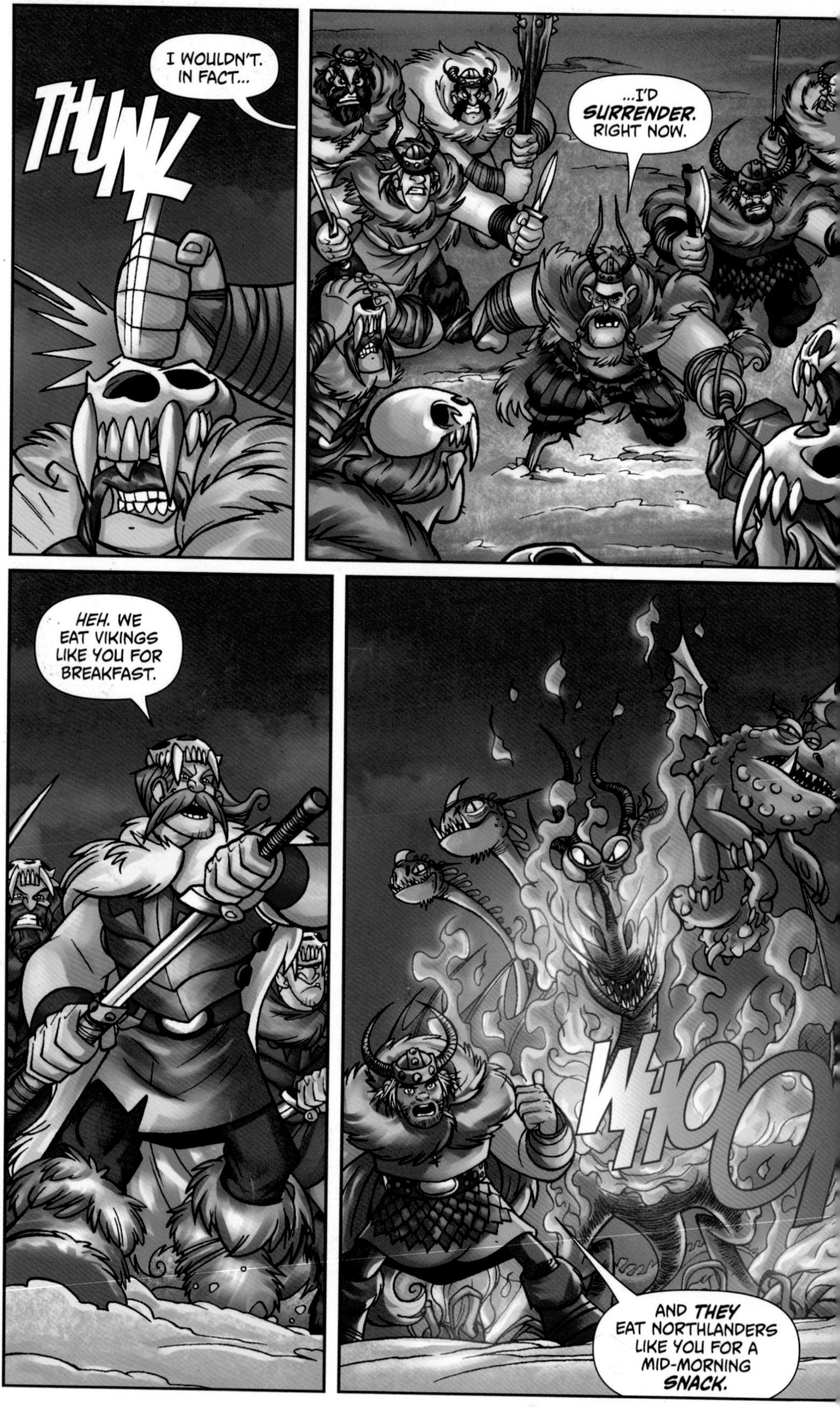
I WOULDN'T. IN FACT...
THUNK
...I'D SURRENDER. RIGHT NOW.
HEH. WE EAT VIKINGS LIKE YOU FOR BREAKFAST.
WHOO
AND THEY EAT NORTHLANDERS LIKE YOU FOR A MID-MORNING SNACK.

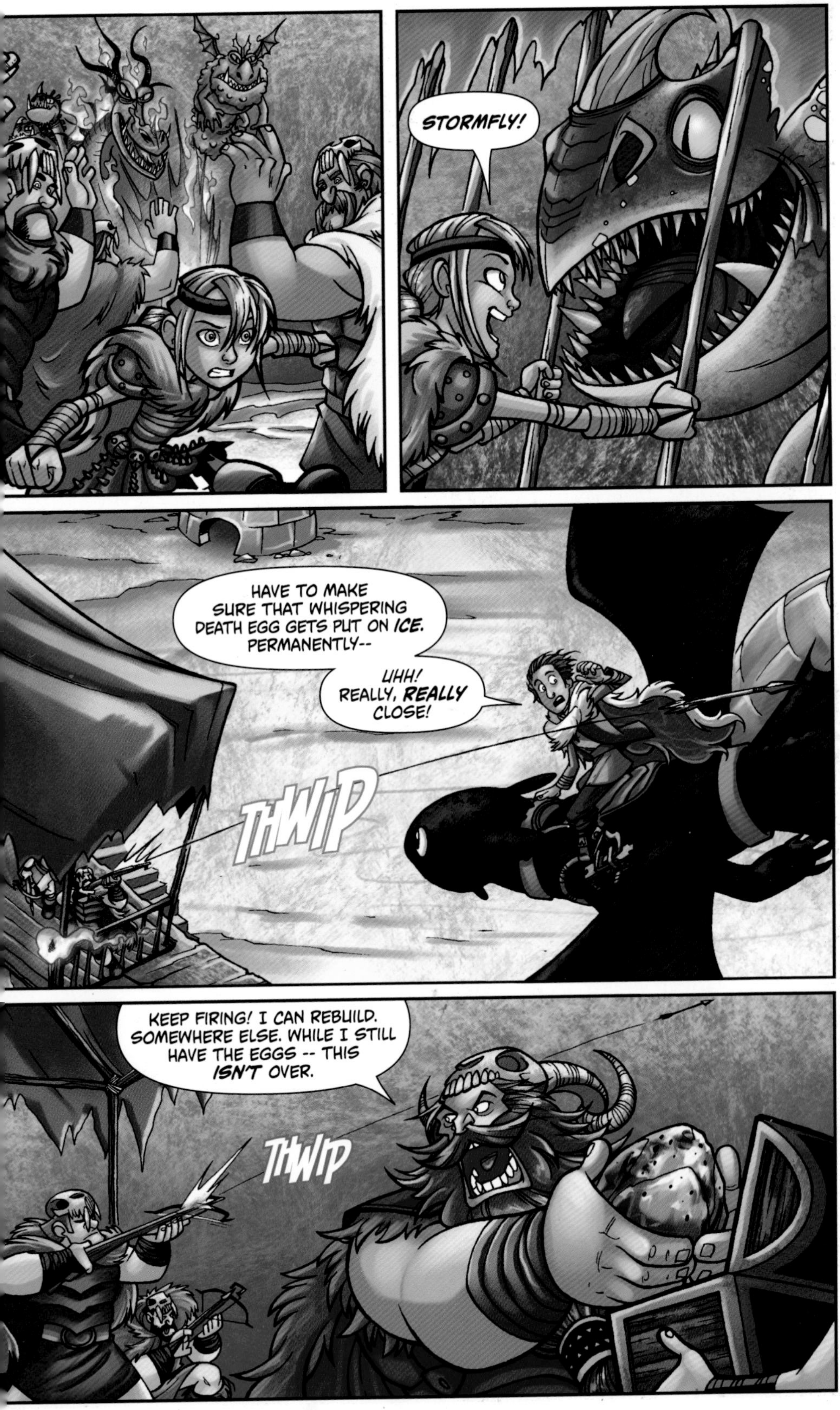
STORMFLY!
HAVE TO MAKE SURE THAT WHISPERING DEATH EGG GETS PUT ON *ICE*. PERMANENTLY--
UHH! REALLY, ***REALLY*** CLOSE!
THWIP
KEEP FIRING! I CAN REBUILD. SOMEWHERE ELSE. WHILE I STILL HAVE THE EGGS -- THIS *ISN'T* OVER.
THWIP

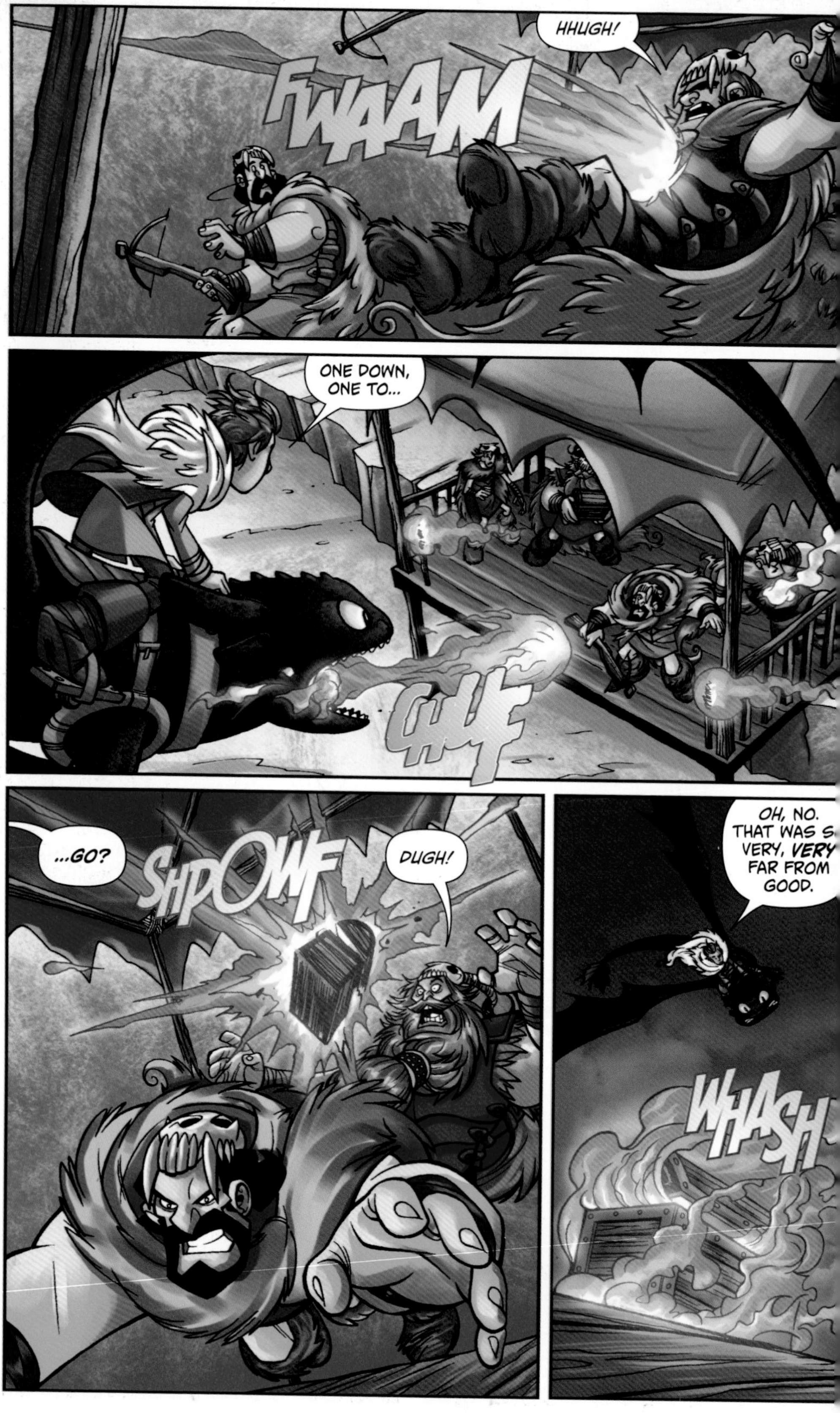
HHUGH!
FWAAM
ONE DOWN, ONE TO...
...GO?
SHPOWF
DUGH!
OH, NO. THAT WAS S
VERY, VERY
FAR FROM GOOD.
WHASH

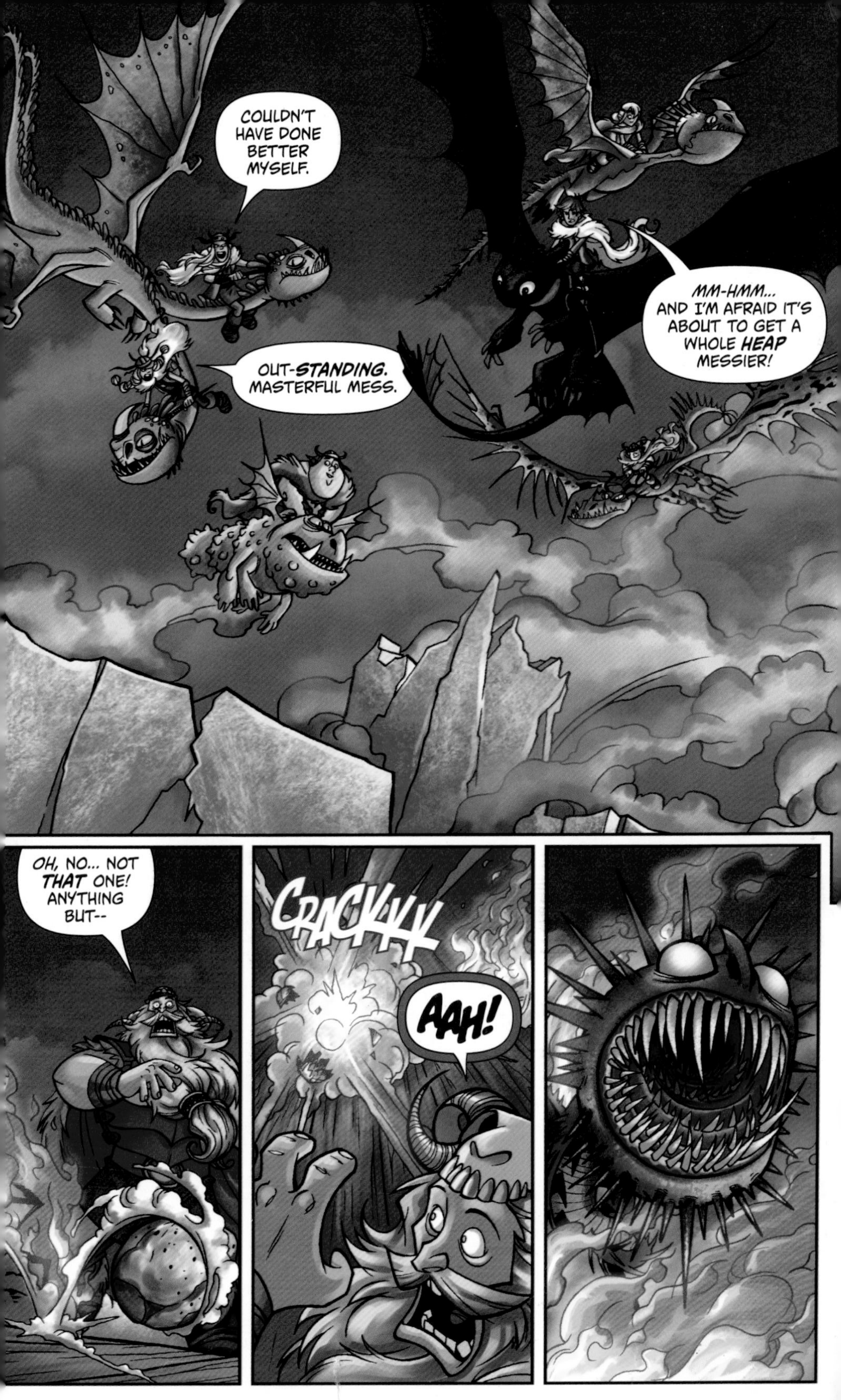
COULDN'T HAVE DONE BETTER MYSELF.
MM-HMM... AND I'M AFRAID IT'S ABOUT TO GET A WHOLE HEAP MESSIER!
OUT-STANDING. MASTERFUL MESS.
OH, NO... NOT THAT ONE! ANYTHING BUT--
CRACKKK
AAH!

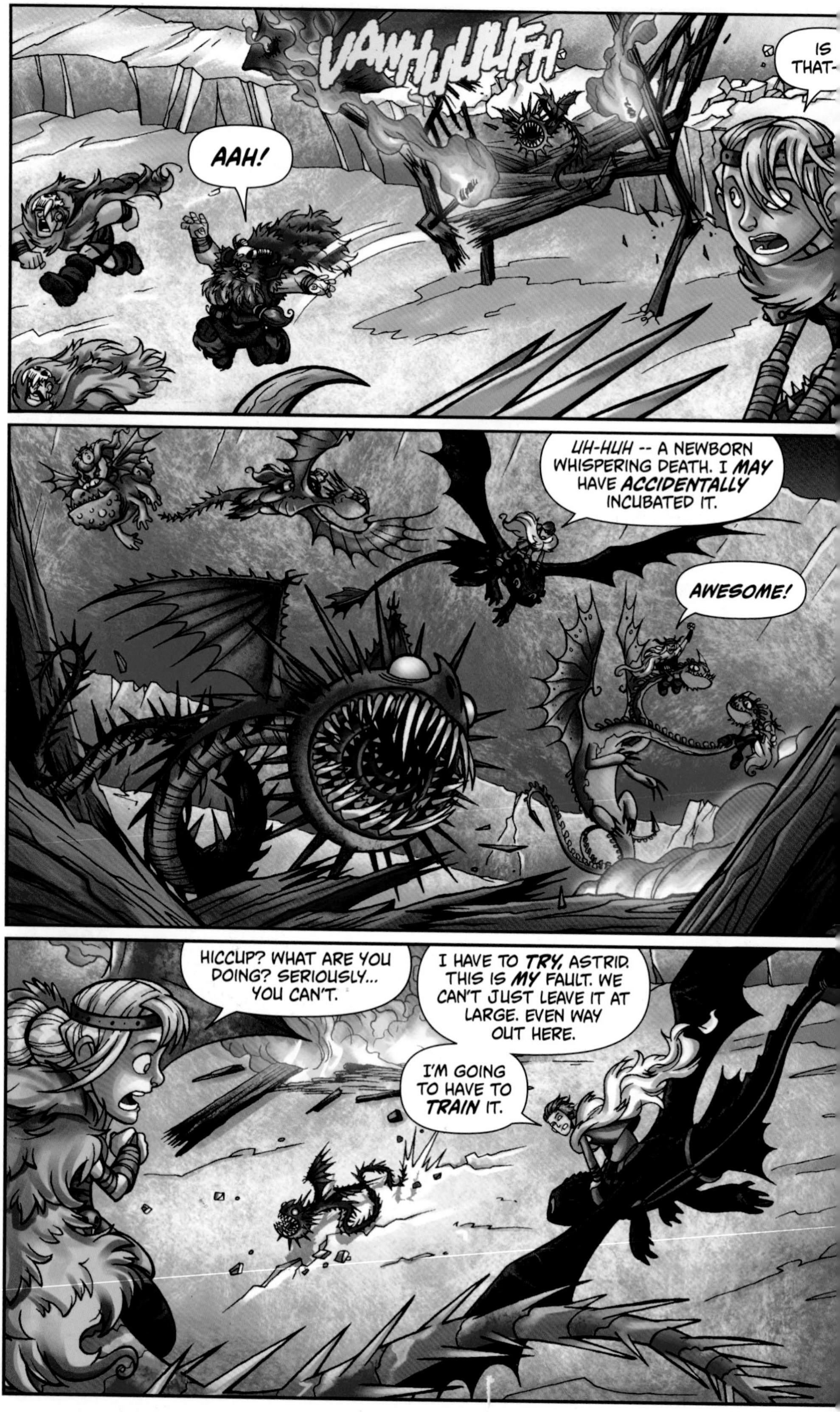
VAWHUUUFH
IS THAT-
AAH!
UH-HUH -- A NEWBORN WHISPERING DEATH. I MAY HAVE ACCIDENTALLY INCUBATED IT.
AWESOME!
HICCUP? WHAT ARE YOU DOING? SERIOUSLY... YOU CAN'T.
I HAVE TO TRY, ASTRID. THIS IS MY FAULT. WE CAN'T JUST LEAVE IT AT LARGE. EVEN WAY OUT HERE.
I'M GOING TO HAVE TO TRAIN IT.

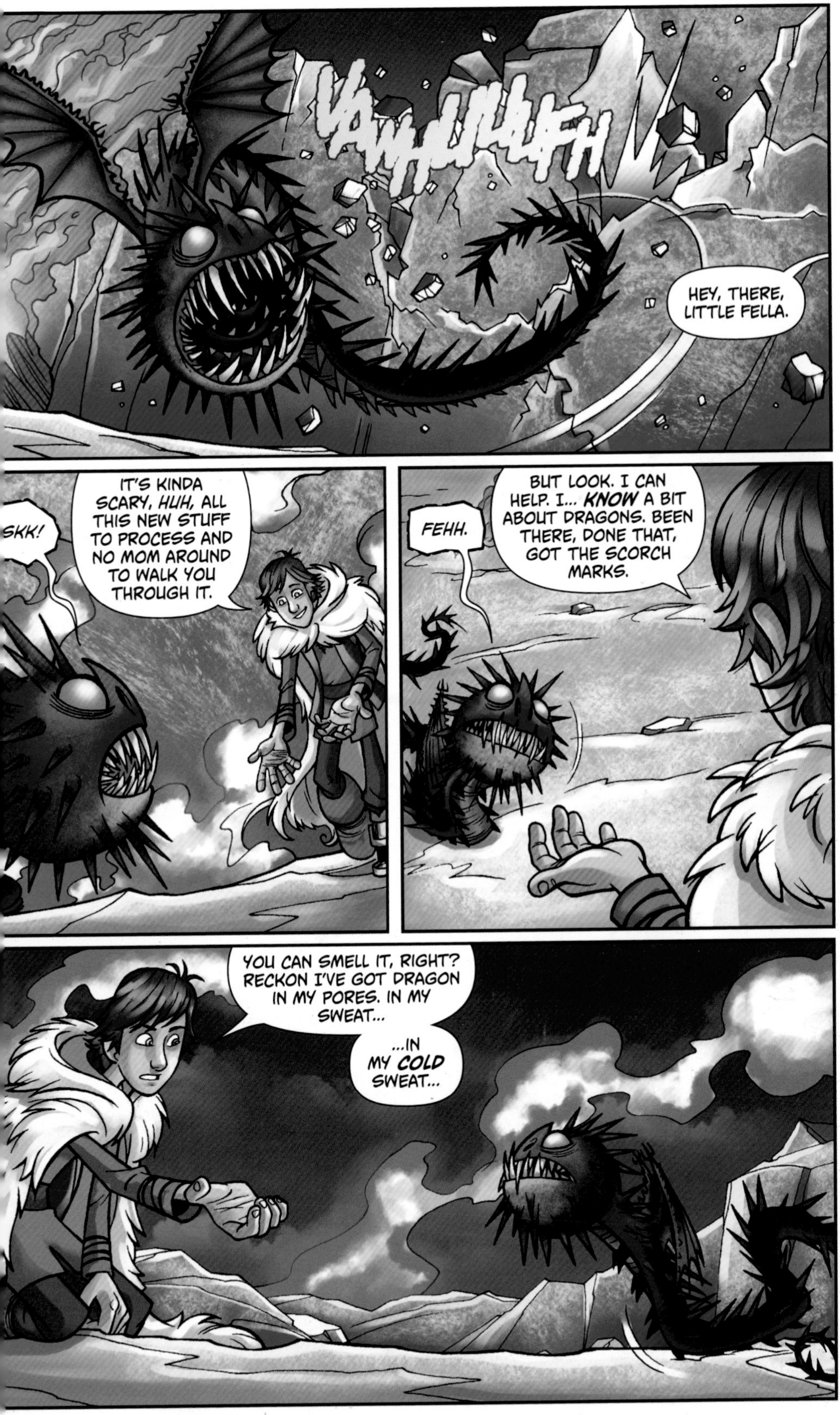
VAWHUUUFH
HEY, THERE, LITTLE FELLA.
SKK!
IT'S KINDA SCARY, HUH, ALL THIS NEW STUFF TO PROCESS AND NO MOM AROUND TO WALK YOU THROUGH IT.
FEHH.
BUT LOOK. I CAN HELP. I... KNOW A BIT ABOUT DRAGONS. BEEN THERE, DONE THAT, GOT THE SCORCH MARKS.
YOU CAN SMELL IT, RIGHT? RECKON I'VE GOT DRAGON IN MY PORES. IN MY SWEAT...
...IN MY COLD SWEAT...

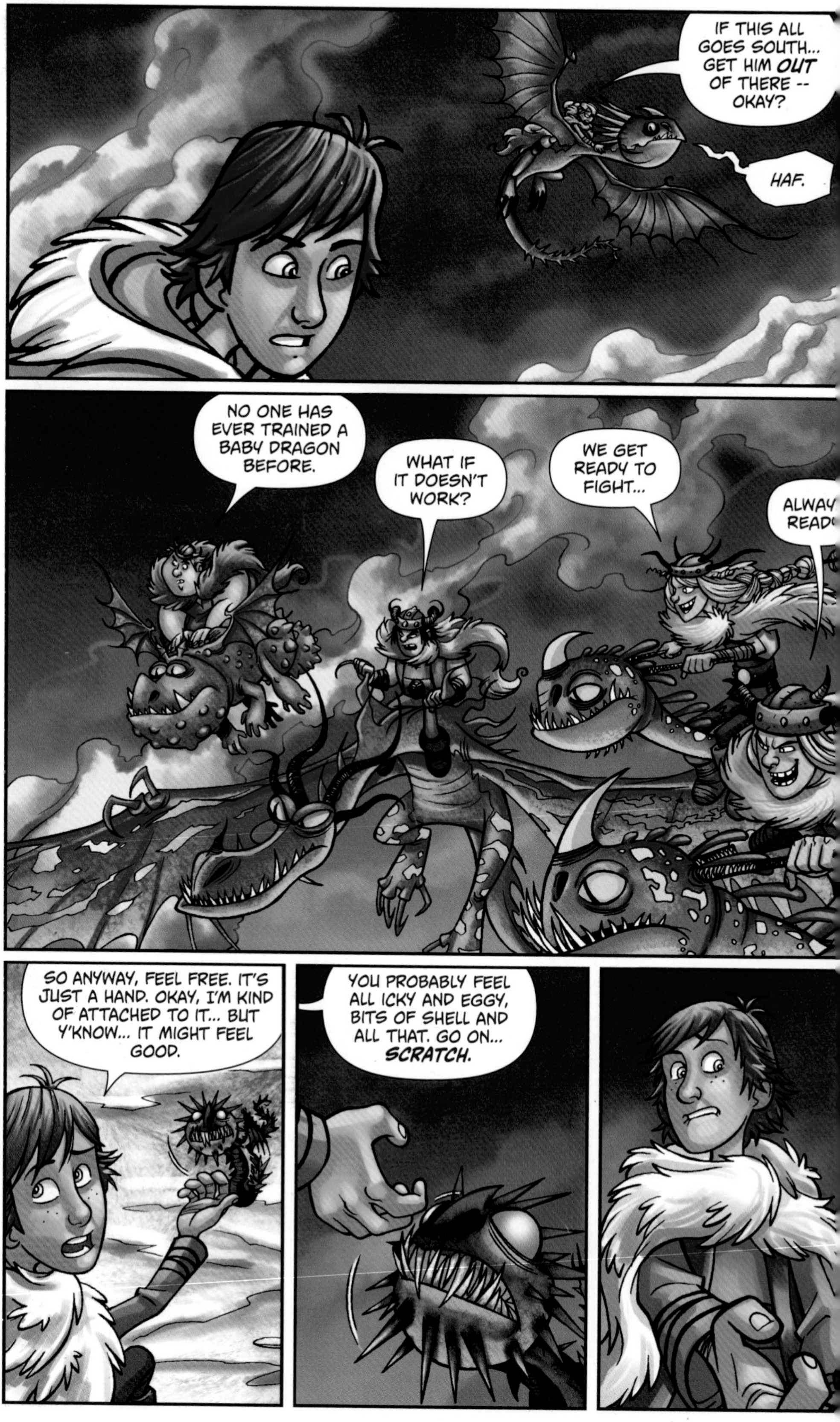
IF THIS ALL GOES SOUTH... GET HIM OUT OF THERE -- OKAY?
HAF.
NO ONE HAS EVER TRAINED A BABY DRAGON BEFORE.
WHAT IF IT DOESN'T WORK?
WE GET READY TO FIGHT...
ALWAY READ
SO ANYWAY, FEEL FREE. IT'S JUST A HAND. OKAY, I'M KIND OF ATTACHED TO IT... BUT Y'KNOW... IT MIGHT FEEL GOOD.
YOU PROBABLY FEEL ALL ICKY AND EGGY, BITS OF SHELL AND ALL THAT. GO ON... SCRATCH.

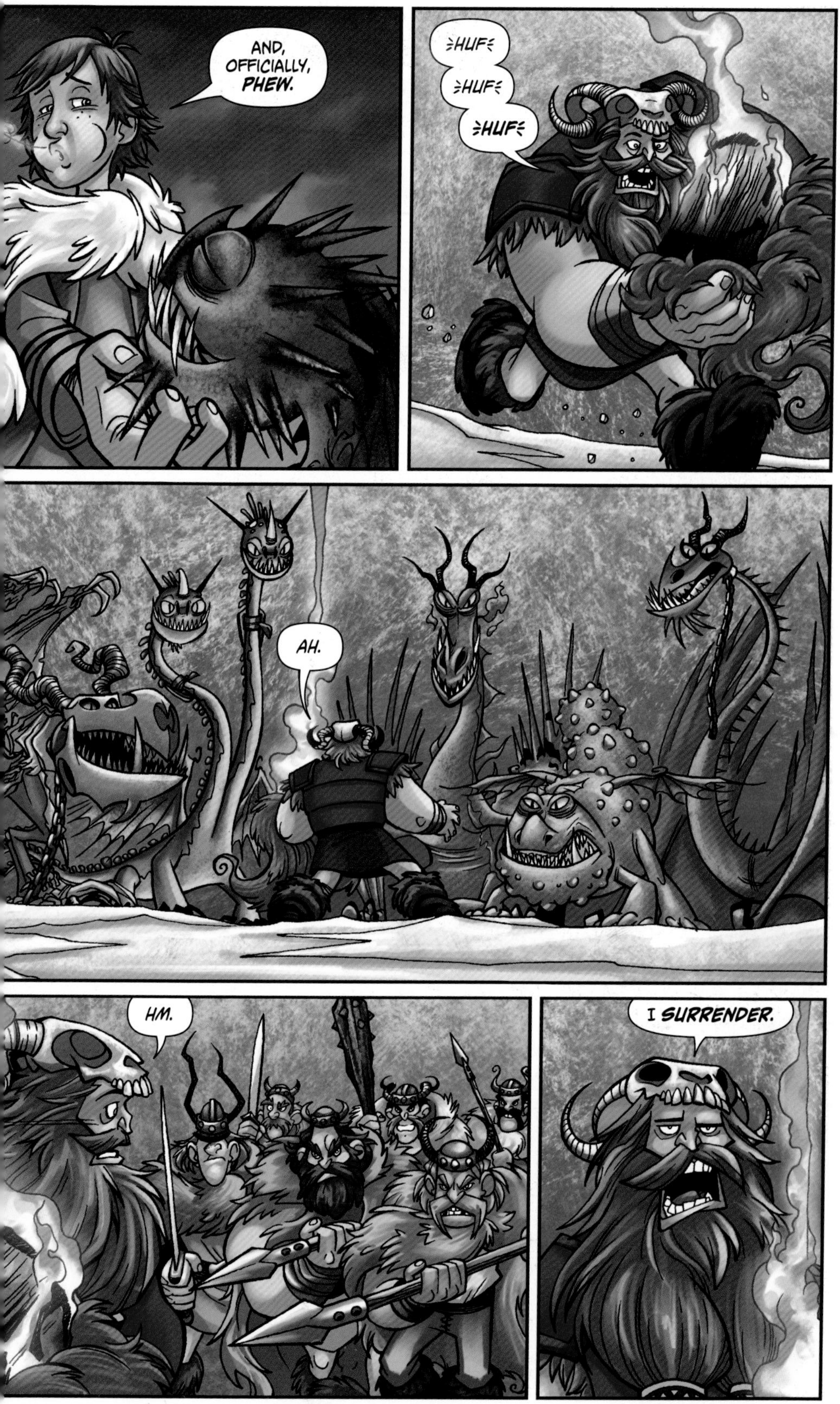
AND, OFFICIALLY, PHEW.
HUF
HUF
HUF
AH.
HM.
I SURRENDER.

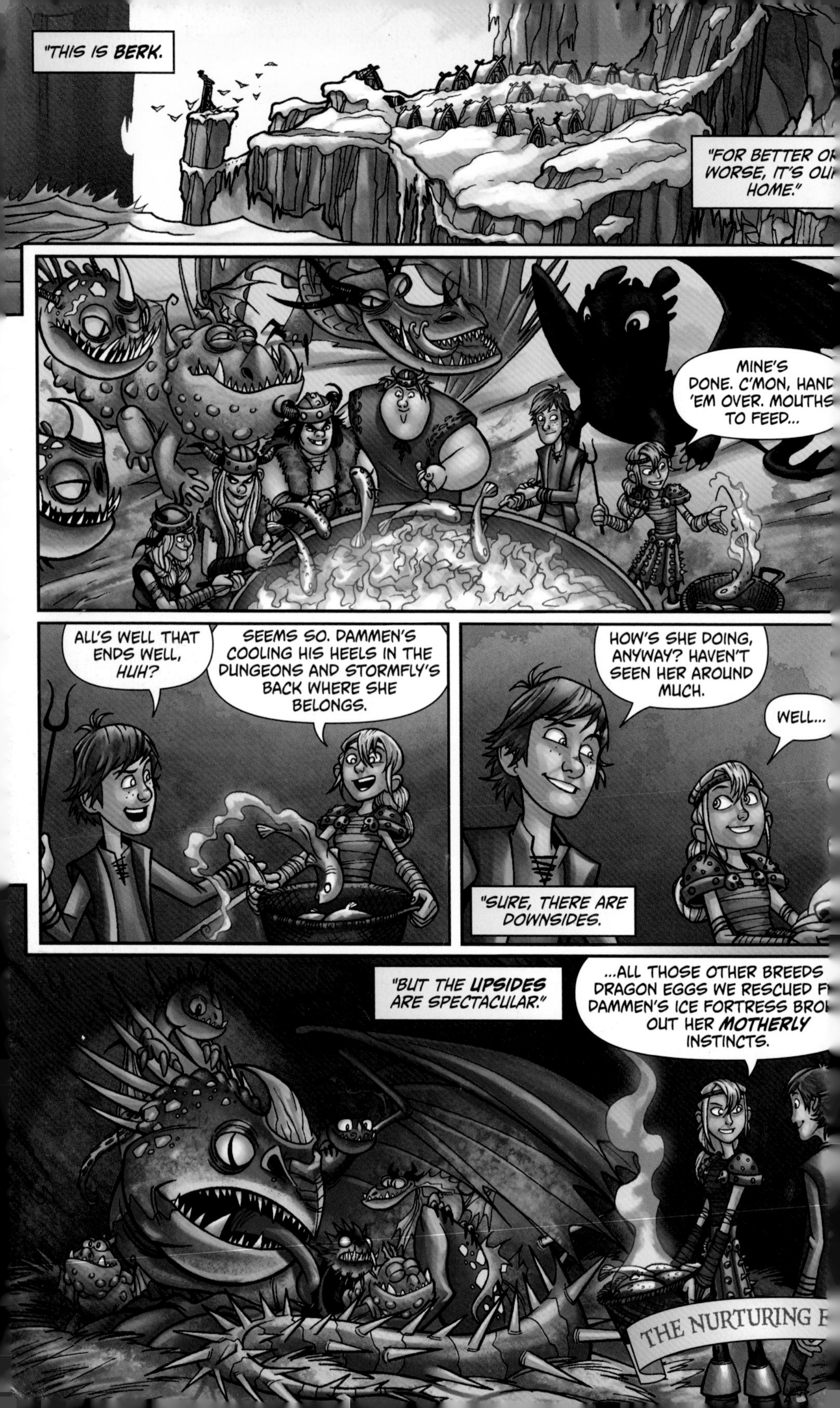
"THIS IS BERK.
"FOR BETTER OR WORSE, IT'S OUR HOME."
MINE'S DONE. C'MON, HAND 'EM OVER. MOUTHS TO FEED...
ALL'S WELL THAT ENDS WELL, HUH?
SEEMS SO. DAMMEN'S COOLING HIS HEELS IN THE DUNGEONS AND STORMFLY'S BACK WHERE SHE BELONGS.
HOW'S SHE DOING, ANYWAY? HAVEN'T SEEN HER AROUND MUCH.
WELL...
"SURE, THERE ARE DOWNSIDES.
"BUT THE UPSIDES ARE SPECTACULAR."
...ALL THOSE OTHER BREEDS DRAGON EGGS WE RESCUED F DAMMEN'S ICE FORTRESS BRO OUT HER MOTHERLY INSTINCTS.
THE NURTURING

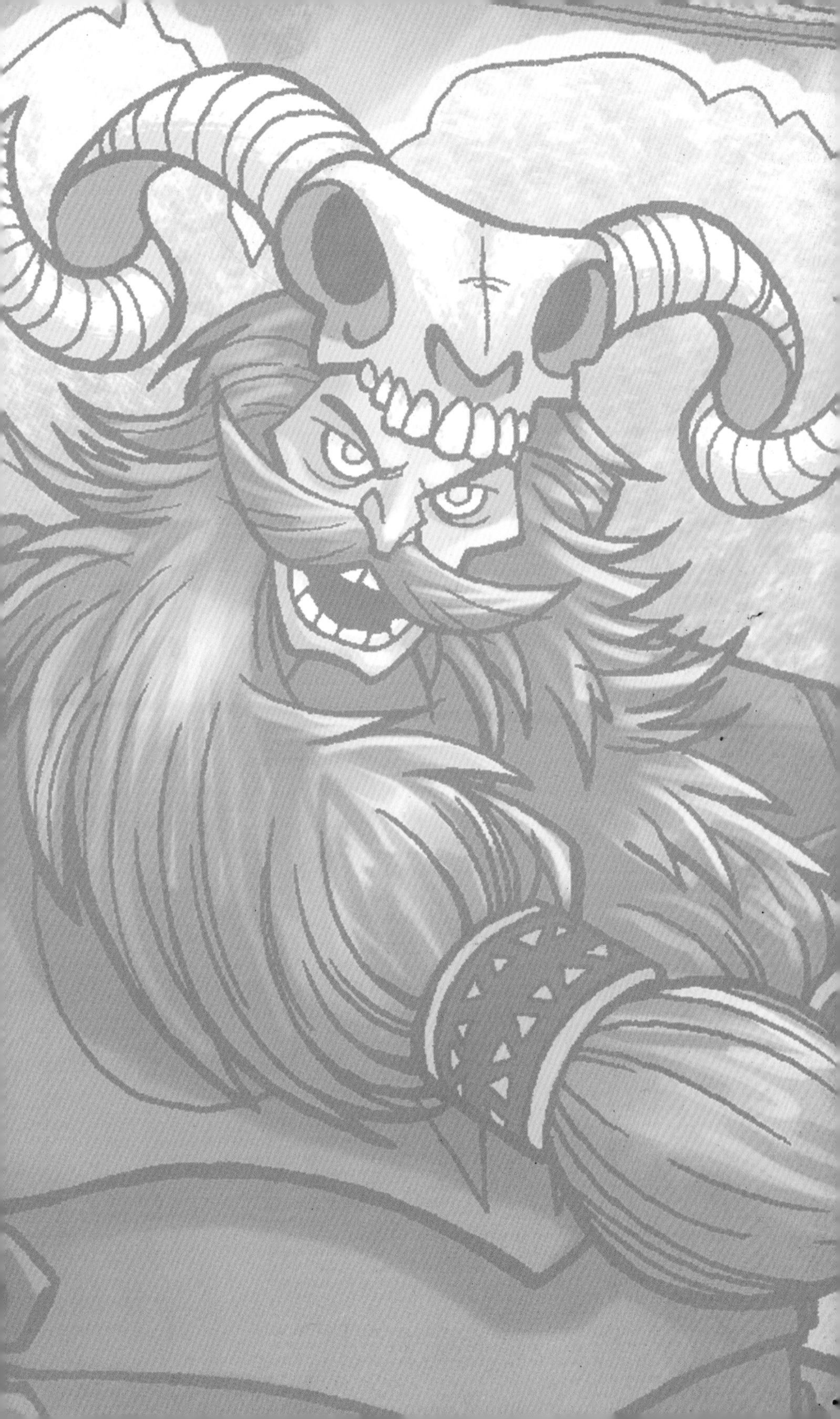

SNOTLOUT IN

LITTER · SITTER

SCRIPT
SIMON FURMAN

ART
STEPHEN DOWNEY

COLORING
JOHN CHARLES

LETTERING
JIM CAMPBELL

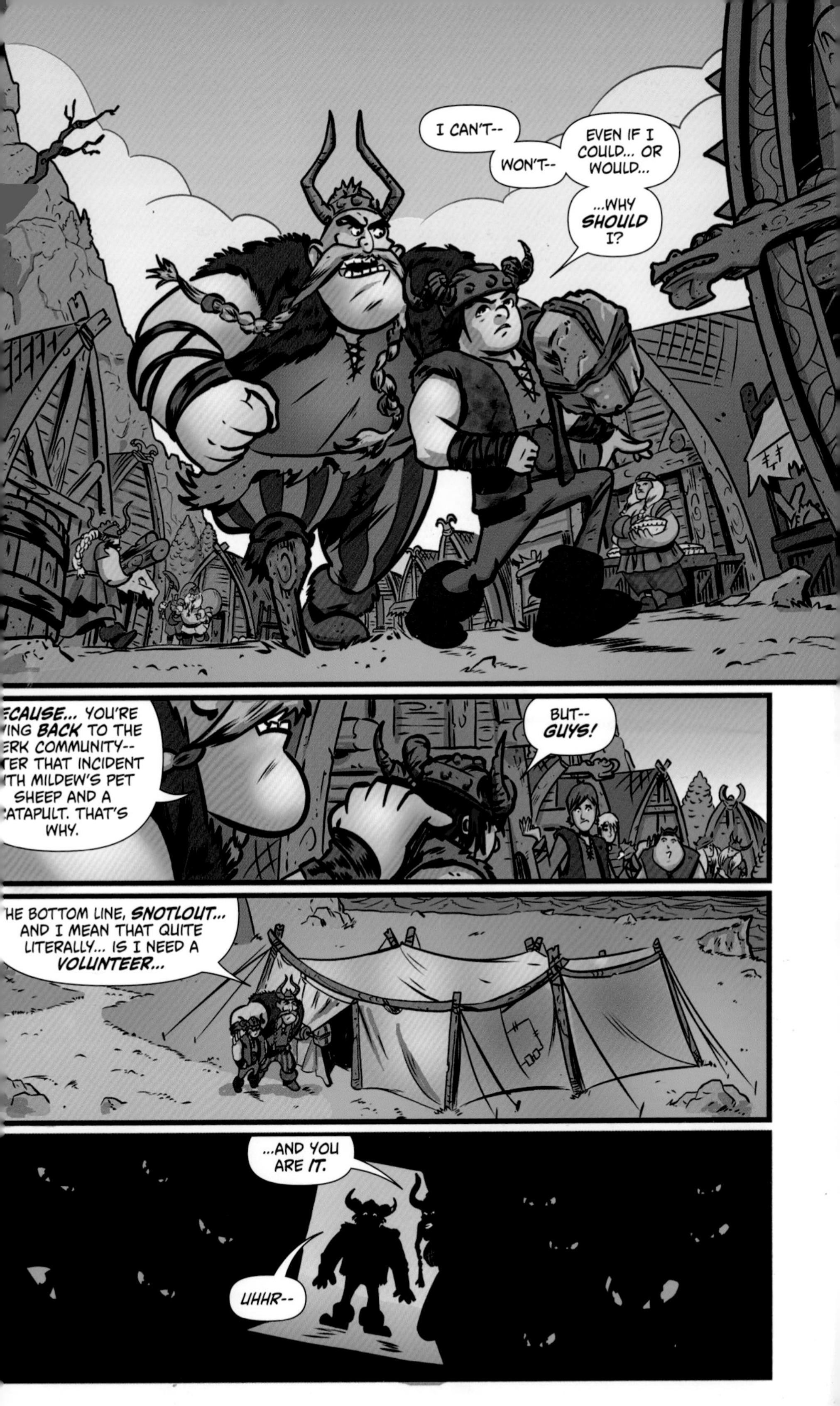
I CAN'T--
WON'T--
EVEN IF I COULD... OR WOULD...
...WHY SHOULD I?
ECAUSE... YOU'RE ING BACK TO THE ERK COMMUNITY-- TER THAT INCIDENT TH MILDEW'S PET SHEEP AND A ATAPULT. THAT'S WHY.
BUT-- GUYS!
HE BOTTOM LINE, SNOTLOUT... AND I MEAN THAT QUITE LITERALLY... IS I NEED A VOLUNTEER...
...AND YOU ARE IT.
UHHR--

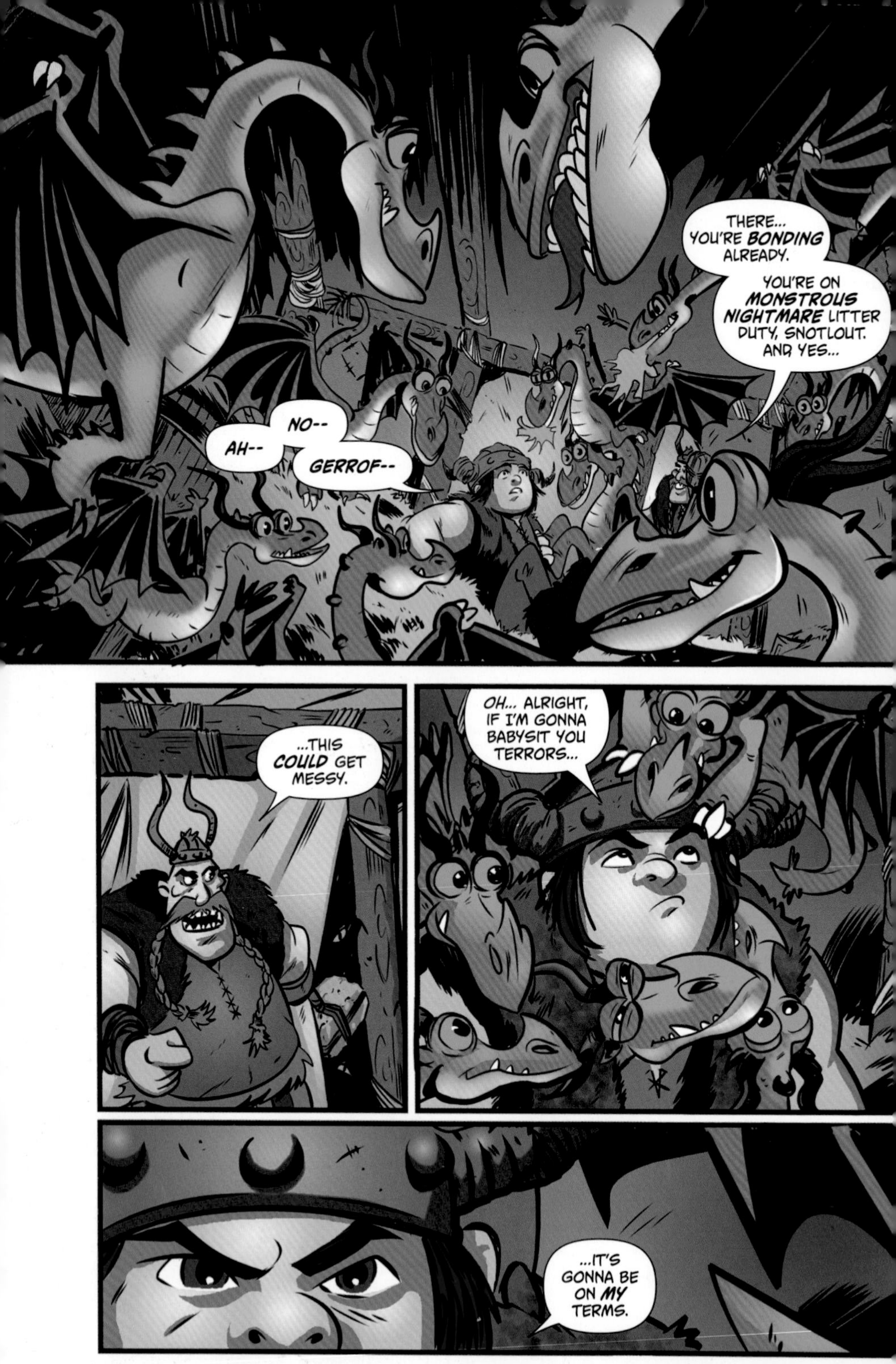
THERE... YOU'RE BONDING ALREADY.
YOU'RE ON MONSTROUS NIGHTMARE LITTER DUTY, SNOTLOUT. AND YES...
NO--
AH--
GERROF--
...THIS COULD GET MESSY.
OH... ALRIGHT, IF I'M GONNA BABYSIT YOU TERRORS...
...IT'S GONNA BE ON MY TERMS.

LITTER · SITTER

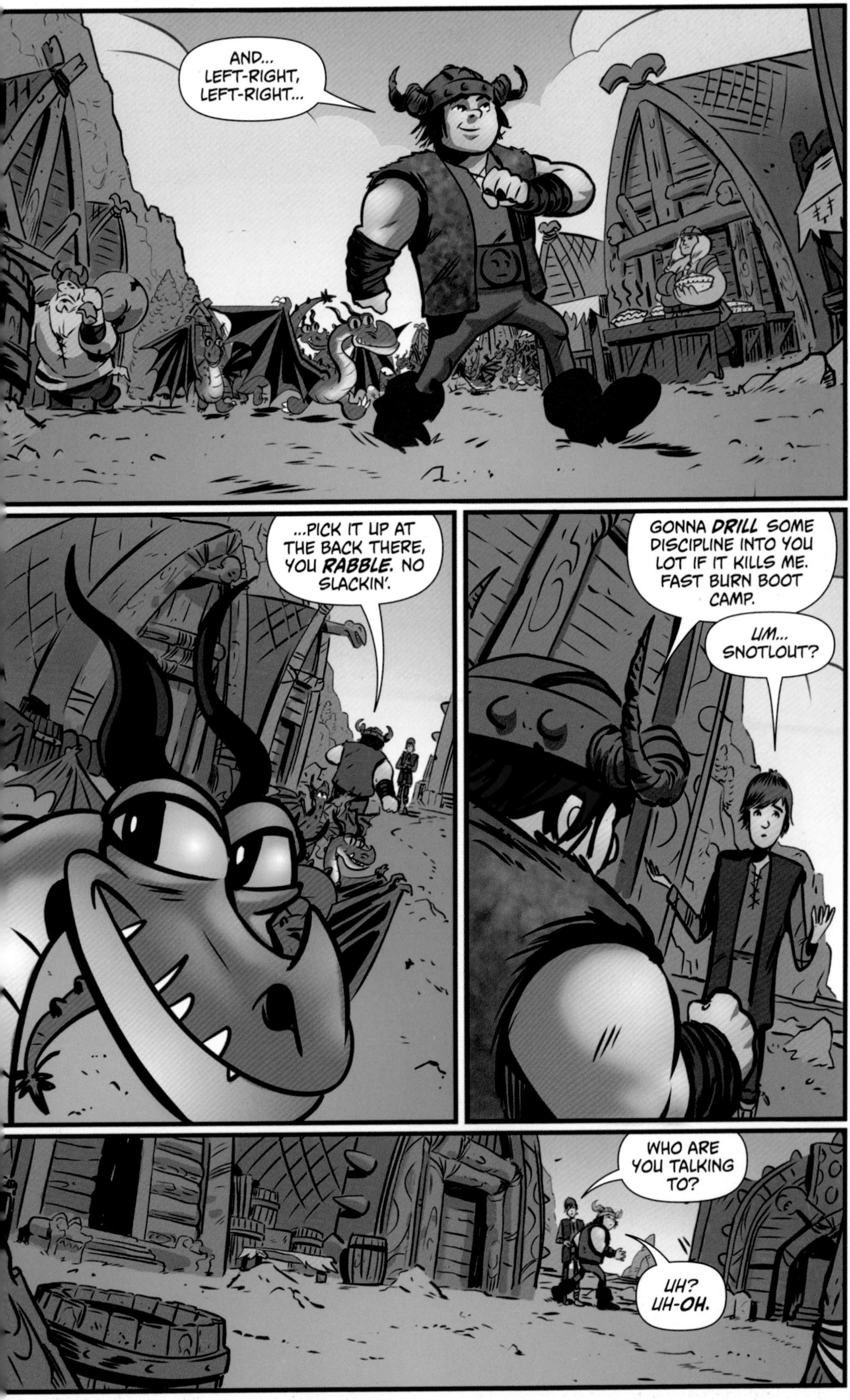
AND... LEFT-RIGHT, LEFT-RIGHT...
...PICK IT UP AT THE BACK THERE, YOU **RABBLE**. NO SLACKIN'.
GONNA **DRILL** SOME DISCIPLINE INTO YOU LOT IF IT KILLS ME. FAST BURN BOOT CAMP.
UM... SNOTLOUT?
WHO ARE YOU TALKING TO?
UH? UH-OH.

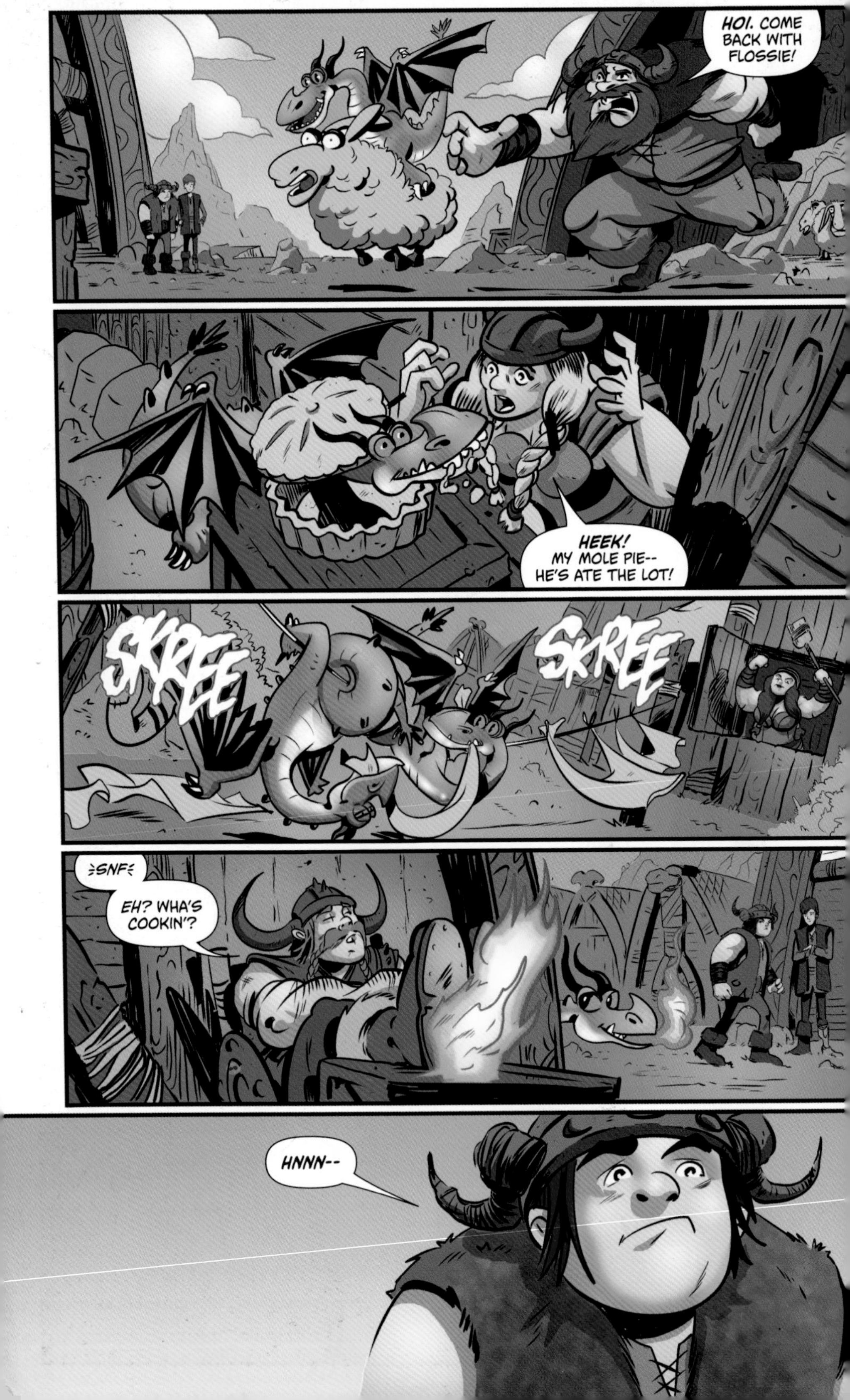
HOI. COME BACK WITH FLOSSIE!
HEEK! MY MOLE PIE-- HE'S ATE THE LOT!
SKREE
SKREE
SNF
EH? WHA'S COOKIN'?
HNNN--

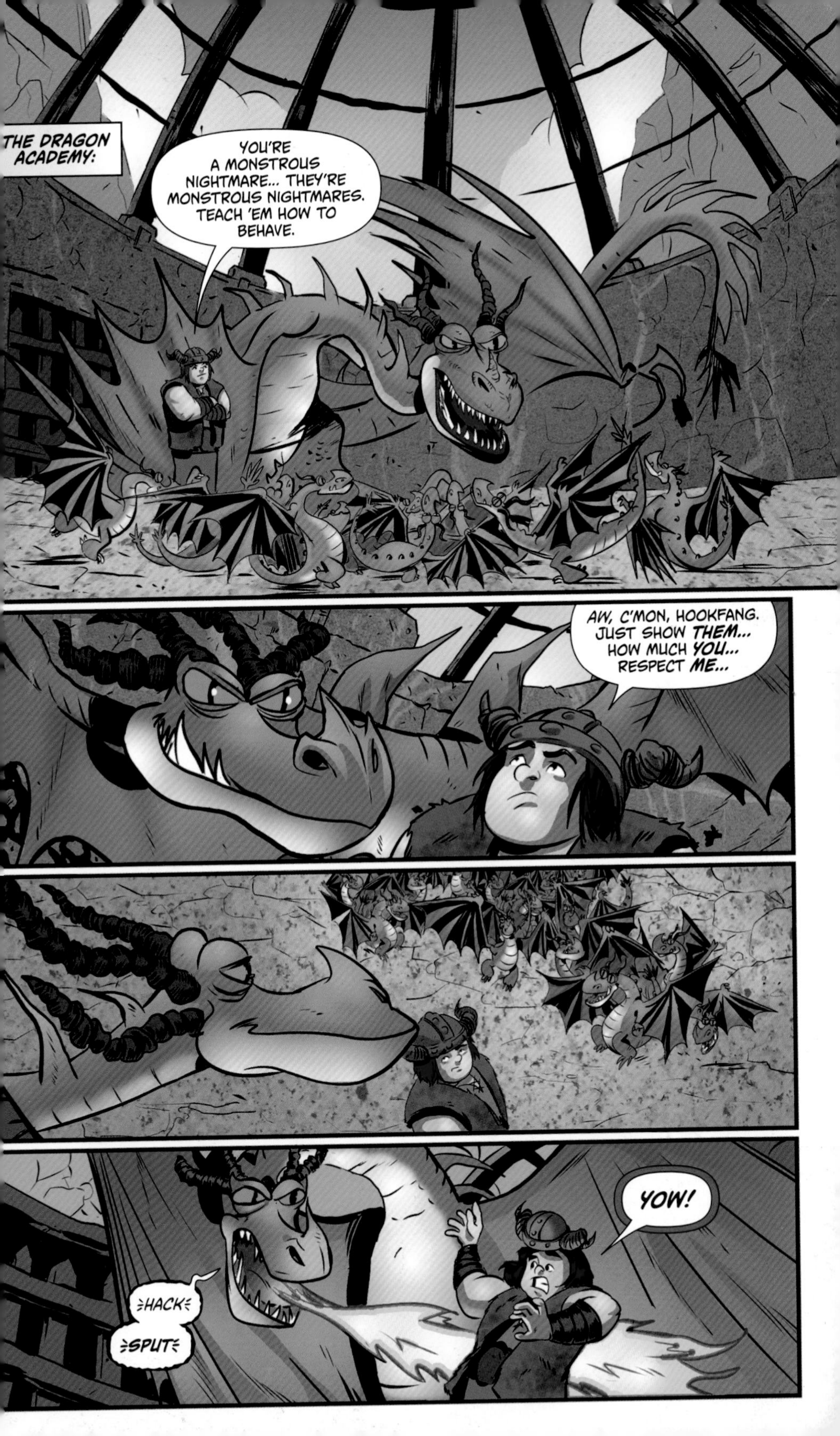
THE DRAGON ACADEMY:
YOU'RE A MONSTROUS NIGHTMARE... THEY'RE MONSTROUS NIGHTMARES. TEACH 'EM HOW TO BEHAVE.
AW, C'MON, HOOKFANG. JUST SHOW THEM... HOW MUCH YOU... RESPECT ME...
YOW!
HACK
SPUT

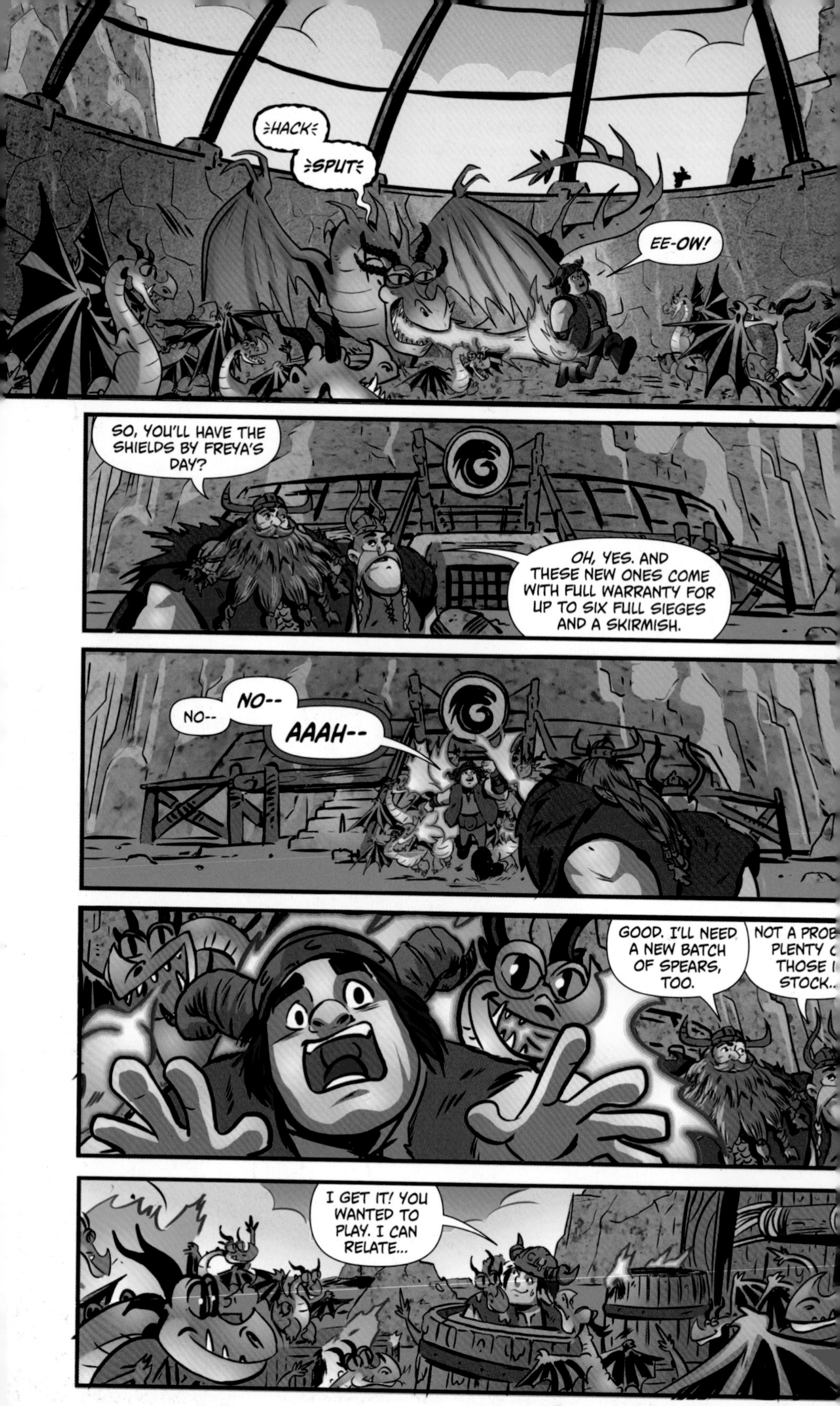
HACK
SPUT
EE-OW!
SO, YOU'LL HAVE THE SHIELDS BY FREYA'S DAY?
OH, YES. AND THESE NEW ONES COME WITH FULL WARRANTY FOR UP TO SIX FULL SIEGES AND A SKIRMISH.
NO--
NO--
AAAH--
GOOD. I'LL NEED A NEW BATCH OF SPEARS, TOO.
I GET IT! YOU WANTED TO PLAY. I CAN RELATE...

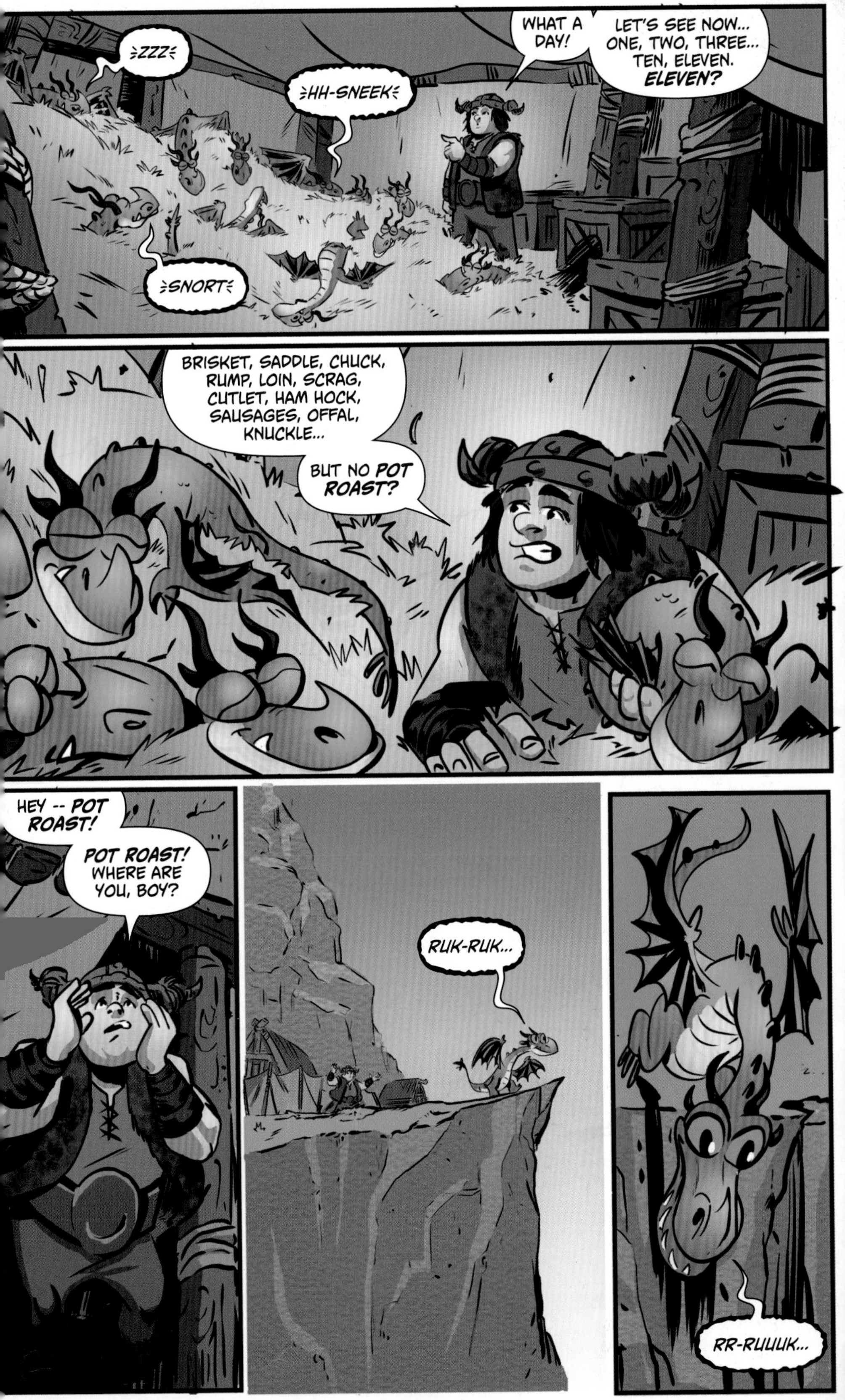
ZZZ
HH-SNEEK
SNORT
WHAT A DAY!
LET'S SEE NOW... ONE, TWO, THREE... TEN, ELEVEN. ELEVEN?
BRISKET, SADDLE, CHUCK, RUMP, LOIN, SCRAG, CUTLET, HAM HOCK, SAUSAGES, OFFAL, KNUCKLE...
BUT NO POT ROAST?
HEY -- POT ROAST!
POT ROAST! WHERE ARE YOU, BOY?
RUK-RUK...
RR-RUUUK...

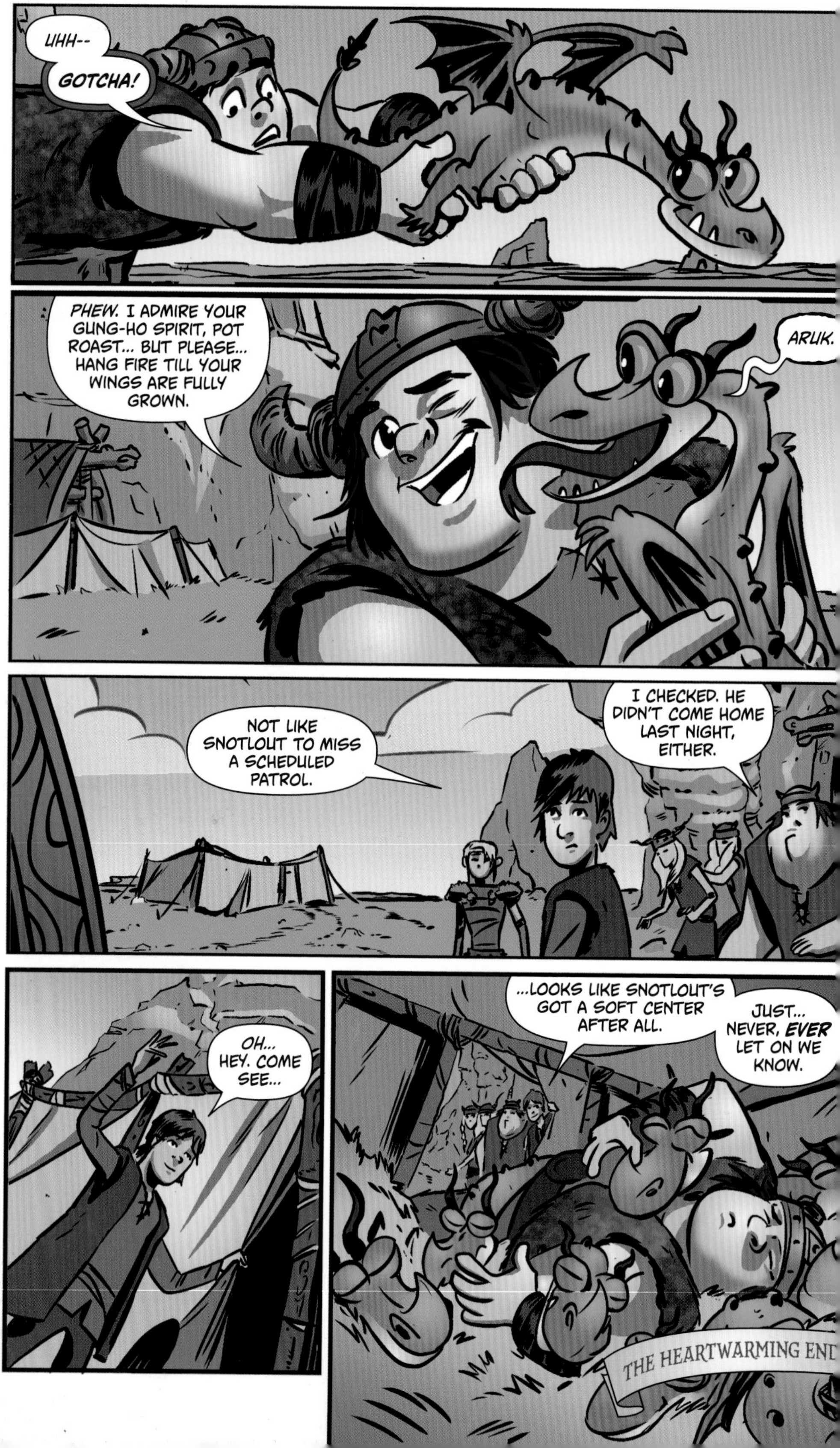
UHH--
GOTCHA!
PHEW. I ADMIRE YOUR GUNG-HO SPIRIT, POT ROAST... BUT PLEASE... HANG FIRE TILL YOUR WINGS ARE FULLY GROWN.
ARUK.
NOT LIKE SNOTLOUT TO MISS A SCHEDULED PATROL.
I CHECKED. HE DIDN'T COME HOME LAST NIGHT, EITHER.
OH... HEY. COME SEE...
...LOOKS LIKE SNOTLOUT'S GOT A SOFT CENTER AFTER ALL.
JUST... NEVER, **EVER** LET ON WE KNOW.
THE HEARTWARMING END

OTHER VOLUMES

DreamWorks
DRAGONS
RIDERS OF BERK
DRAGON DOWN

DreamWorks
DRAGONS
RIDERS OF BERK
VOLUME 4

DreamWorks
DRAGONS
RIDERS OF BERK
VOLUME 5

ON SALE NOW - VOLUME ONE: DRAGON DOWN

Snotlout's dragon, Hookfang, goes missing and a search party is organized... Unfortunately, Alvin the Treacherous is also on the hunt for Hookfang... Who will get to Hookfang first...?

COMING SOON!

VOLUME FOUR
(Available March 3, 2015)

VOLUME FIVE
(Available May 5, 2015)

VOLUME SIX
(Available July 7, 2015)

For more information visit www.titancomics.com

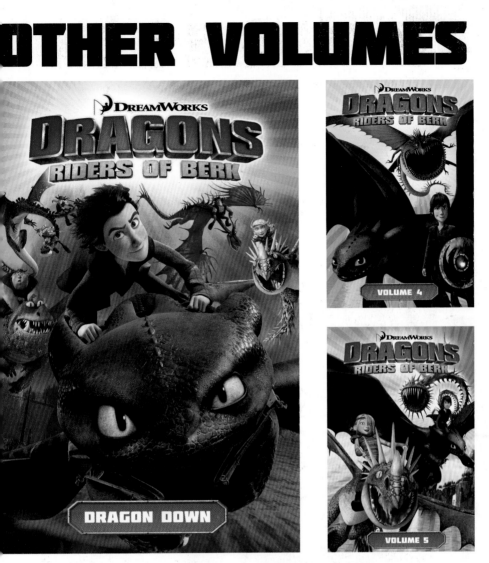

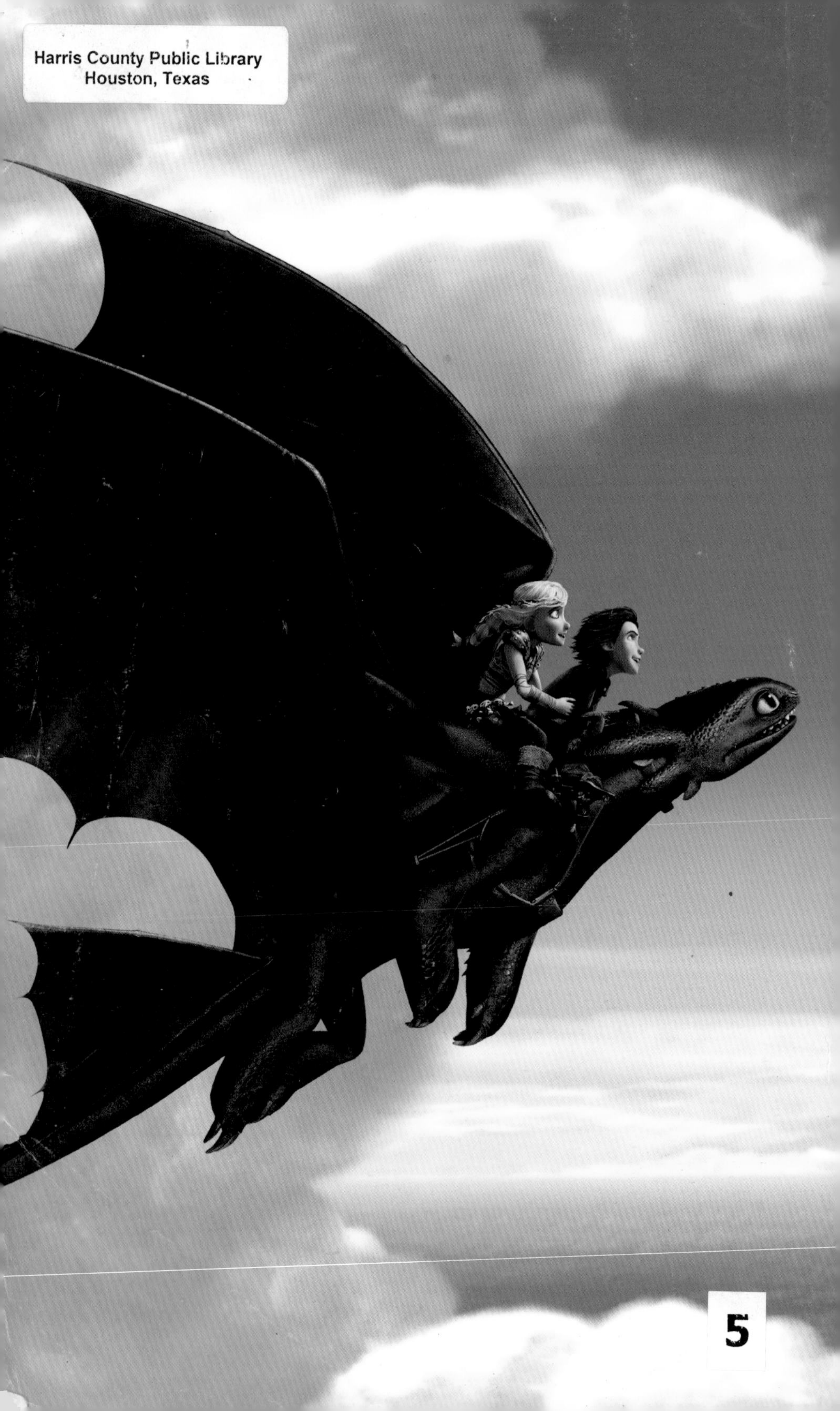
5